The Lamentations of Blackhawk

T.J. TRANCHELL

LAST DAYS BOOKS

Email the author at: tj.tranchell@gmail.com

Website: www.tjtranchell.net

"The Lamentations of Blackhawk" Printing History
Last Days Books paperback edition November 2022

ISBN: 979-8-218-08593-3

Printed in the United States of America
www.tjtranchell.net

PRAISE FOR...

CRY DOWN DARK:

"This is the kind of knife-edge story that will keep you up at night, startling at every noise."
— *New York Times*

ASLEEP IN THE NIGHTMARE ROOM:

"If you enjoy horror but want to try something a little different, I definitely recommend this inspired, personal, and thought provoking collection."
— Jennifer Soucy, author of *Demon in Me*, *The Night She Fell*, and *Clementine's Awakening*

THE PRIVATE LIVES OF NIGHTMARES:

"Tranchell flaunts his literary chops once more with further proof of both his fiction and nonfiction abilities."
— Michelle von Eschen, author of *Old Farmhouses of the North*, *Mistakes I Made During the Zombie Apocalypse*, *When You Find Out What You're Made Of*, and others

TELL NO MAN:

"It's creepy, fast, and the right kind of gory."
— Gabino Iglesias, author of *Zero Saints* and *Coyote Songs*

ALSO BY T.J. TRANCHELL

THE BLACKHAWK CYCLE:
Cry Down Dark
Tell No Man

COLLECTIONS:
Asleep in the Nightmare Room
The Private Lives of Nightmares

FOR THOM CARNELL

"He hath set me in dark places, as they
that be dead of old."
Lamentations 3:6 KJV

CHAPTER ONE

Brandon Smith prayed for anyone caught in the canyon when the fire raged to life. He had the TV on KSL 5, watching the coverage of the fire raging down Blackhawk Canyon, toward the homes at the mouth of the canyon. His favorite spot, Beer Can Flats, and the Boy Scout camp Maple Dell had already been consumed by the flames. The small lakes, the news said, were boiling and any fish in them would be dead. They had nowhere to go.

David, his brother, watched live trail camera footage online from cameras attached to the Aspen trees carefully placed to spot deer, elk, wild turkeys, and once, a bear. The bear had been on KSL, which is how they knew about the website with the cameras. Usually, they only saw small birds and chipmunks. If the bear still lived in the canyon, it had probably already died. The rush of deer and elk past the camera thrilled David, but not because he enjoyed seeing the wildlife anymore. He watched the beasts running for their lives and laughed, hoping he would see the flames catch up to a slow deer. He wasn't given that satisfaction; the cameras soon burned, and the feeds were lost. People camping in the woods above Blackhawk lost tents, RVs, backpacks, lives. No humans ran past the cameras before the site went dark.

Some of the animals David watched came down the hills and into town. Had Brandon known more, he would have prayed for the evil that came out of the woods with the animals and the fire to stay there. He'd had enough of fire.

But he didn't know.

David did not pray with his brother. When the live feeds became static and then just blackness, he thought of the suffering of the animals he had seen and that of people he felt sure had been engulfed in flames. Limbs—human and tree alike—turned to cinders. A laugh swelled inside him, but like the burning core that had grown in his guts for months now, he kept it down.

He did know. He knew this wouldn't be the last fire to burn through Blackhawk.

The thing inside him, the thing making him laugh and burn, stayed quiet. It had only told one person it was there and only one time—when the man with the black gloves first knocked on David's door. It didn't let David remember that. Instead, it filled David's insides with ashes and his dreams with fiery glory, a glory that would come when it decided it was time to reveal itself again.

The fire, though, was hard to resist. It wanted to be there, to run with the flames of its comrades and devour more than just the bowels of this boy. The boy sometimes fed it flesh, but always dead flesh, never fresh. Never screaming for mercy.

Then it heard something different from the noise box the other fleshmeat worshipped. And it knew the time was soon.

***

Another dry summer followed another harsh and late winter. Once the heat struck Utah in May, the thirsty sky sucked up all the moisture in the ground and from the trees, leaving just enough in the ponds and reservoirs to avoid a state of emergency. All around town, lawns died while folks huddled under air conditioners and watched the news of fires in California and Oregon and Washington. Fires that didn't affect them; fires whose smoke blew north instead of east; fires that burned the homes of strangers and not of their families.

All summer, Maddie Smith watched fires in other states instead of politics, sometimes even forgetting her sons, just to forget everything from the previous summer. Blackhawk sat smack in the middle of conservative Utah and there was no use telling your neighbor you voted for someone else because they and your other four neighbors voted for the same old Republicans over and over. They never needed to talk politics at church because everyone voted straight GOP because white men in power reflected the church itself.

In Blackhawk, like in most small towns, what one saw on the surface was rarely all there was to see. Even some of the church buildings were unique. There's the old green church, like a reject from the Emerald City because it wasn't quite green enough, and the square, steepleless building in the center of town where the Smiths attended services before they moved across town. There had been talk about turning part of the parking lot into a memorial for two men—one a former bishop of this ward—who had died the previous summer. Blaine Griffen had died with three other men in a house fire—so much fire, Maddie thought again—and the other at the cemetery. Brandon Smith had been the only surviving witness of the house fire and the authorities still wondered why they'd all been there. Maddie and Brandon— although he doesn't remember much of that day—were the only people with Rey Montoya when he suffered a heart attack at the Blackhawk Cemetery. More questions than answers, and none of the answers seemed to fit what the police wanted to hear. No foul play from Maddie or Brandon had been suspected, but when nothing seemed to fit, things were brushed under the rug, as is the nature of small towns.

The church liked things quiet, too, but did not let go as easily.

Listening for the sounds of her boys, Maddie sat outside in the worst of the summer August heat, watching the smoke billow, praying for the friends she knew who'd been evacuated, praying that the fires would not come nearer to her home, praying that the flames could be stopped. She had had enough of fire.

As she watched a helicopter making its run over the canyon, she heard a rustling at the back of her property. Through the trees peered a small deer. Maddie remained still. She thought briefly of the pansies she had planted a few weeks earlier and decided if the flowers could feed this lost animal, she could just get more. The deer moved slowly but gracefully into Maddie's yard and toward the small purple flowers. Maddie sat transfixed by the animal, not wanting to spook it, wondering where it would go if she did.

She did not hear the sliding glass door open behind her and heard nothing until David screamed and ran toward the deer. The animal froze for a moment before sprinting forward and jumping over the fence into the neighbor's yard.

"David," Maddie said. "Why did you do that?"

Her youngest son stood in front of her, his back toward her, now as still as the deer had been before entering the yard. She heard a popping sound, mistaking it for the sound of trees bursting into flames, before realizing the sound came from David. His feet still pointed away from her, but his chest and face had turned in her direction. He lifted an arm, pointing a finger at her while also walking away.

"It's your fault, Maddie," came a croaking voice out of David's mouth. "This is all your fault, bitch." He walked to the spot where the deer had been, still facing her and pointing. His other arm reached behind—in front?—his back and she saw the motions of him unzipping his pants. Looking at her, pointing and laughing, David urinated on her flowers.

She closed her eyes, wanting to scream but not wanting to alarm anyone nearby. When she opened her eyes, David, his body facing all the natural directions but with his fly still open and a runnel of blood worming out of his nose, lay on the ground. His eyes fluttered and a smile remained on his face, but thankfully he had stopped laughing.

A new scream belched from inside the house and the ground began to tremble. Maddie could do nothing but fall to her knees and pray.

***

Later, Maddie told her boys about the first time she'd felt an earthquake. She had been up north, swimming in Bear Lake, with her parents and extended family. Someone had told her about the Bear Lake Monster and how it loved to grab ten-year-old girls by the legs and shake them until they drowned. Then the monster would eat them. "It's a kindness," her cousin had said, "that the monster never eats anyone alive." A dozen people had drowned in the lake since he'd been born, according the wiser, older, twelve-year-old boy. Whole bodies were never recovered, just pieces.

"I remember that the most," Maddie said. "That only pieces—a hand, a foot, two arms that didn't match, according to my cousin Rob—floated up, never a whole body."

She'd laughed but when the waves grew larger and the shore seemed to ripple, Maddie gulped water and felt like she was being pulled into a blender. Her dad snatched her out of the water while she kept her eyes closed, expecting instead to feel the claws of the beast rather than the rough but gentle hand of her father. She didn't see her family running to nowhere, some hiding beneath cars—"That's what you do during a tornado, moron!" she heard—most staying in the open. She managed to cough out the water she'd swallowed onto her dad's back and by the time he'd lowered her onto a towel, the tremors had ceased.

"This isn't helping, Mom," Brandon said, clutching his knees to his chest.

She smiled at him, only half-forced. *Lord, how he's grown. David, too. I missed a whole summer and now this one is nearly gone*, she thought.

"The monster was probably just hungry," David said. He had taken the floor, laid out flat on his stomach, his head away from Maddie and Brandon. "You can't be mad at something if it's just hungry."

"David, are you okay?" Maddie said. He hadn't spoken a word since she'd brought him into the living room from the backyard. He'd stared, blank-eyed, as she scrubbed the blood off his lip and nose, not moving or making a sound. When she'd finished, he'd found his spot on the floor and only momentarily did it appear he was even listening.

"Yeah, Mom. I'm cool."

Dipping her eyes toward Brandon, she motioned for him to say something to his brother.

"That new Avengers movie will be out on disc, soon. You want to watch it with me, dude?" Brandon said.

"Who wins?" David asked back.

"We'll have to watch it to find out."

"We should watch this instead," David said. He raised the remote and turned the volume back up on the TV. An ad for CSI reruns ended and the news returned.

KSL continues its coverage of the wildfires throughout the state and now breaking news regarding the 5.7 earthquake that rocked Salt Lake City and the surrounding area less than an hour ago.

Footage here appears to show the trumpet portion of the Angel Moroni statue atop the Salt Lake Temple falling from the hands of the statue. Cracks at the base of the 128-year-old temple formed during the peak of the quake. Total damages at the landmark building have yet to be assessed and no word from Church officials has been given.

"Oh, Jesus," Maddie blurted. David sat up, legs crossed, engrossed in the repeated frames of the trumpet falling. Brandon stayed as he was, knees to chest, breathing heavily.

Rumors among members of The Church of Jesus Christ of Latter-day Saints that the falling of the trumpet and damage to the temple serve as a sign of the "end times" are expected to be quelled by officials once a statement is released.

"She's wrong. Look," David said. He pointed out the window, to the view of the Blackhawk Temple, less than five years old itself. Then his voice changed again, taking a pitch much lower than a ten-year-old boy's should be. "The end is coming. All things on Earth and in Heaven shall tremble and become ruin."

With the glow of flames beyond the cream-hued temple, Maddie watched as the entire Angel Moroni statue fell from the spire and crashed onto the parking lot beneath it. She couldn't hear the car alarms but imagined the blaring from the half-dozen smashed vehicles.

Brandon didn't look outside. He watched as the news turned to temples throughout the state suffer shattered windows and falling statuary.

Reports are coming in from across the state that temples, even more recently built temples, are taking heavy damage from aftershocks. A viewer has sent us this video of the windows of the Logan Temple bursting outward. Parents, if you have children watching, you may want to avert their eyes as a group of young men and women were outside the building at the time of the aftershock. We will continue our co...

Maddie stepped on the remote control, causing the TV to shut off. "We've been through enough, haven't we?" Sitting in front of David, she grasped him by the shoulders. "Haven't we been through enough? Let us go, damn you. Leave us alone!" She stopped herself from shaking David and wrapped him in a hug. Brandon joined them, his arms reaching now almost all the way around his mother and younger brother.

"We should call Peter," Brandon said.

CHAPTER TWO

Peter Toombs, lately of Los Angeles, California; Bern, Utah; and Reno, Nevada; but always from Blackhawk, Utah; sits on the shore of Moon Lake in a tattered director's chair, directing nothing. Beside him stands a Canon EOS R5 atop a starkly black tripod. Beneath the chair, the dark lumps of the equipment bag and a bag full of soda and snack wait for him to decide it was time to eat or time to leave.

With the camera off, he rehearses his narration, finding the right pace between his hero Rod Serling and that usurper with the Hobbit name who'd taken over Skinwalker Ranch a few miles south of Moon Lake. Toombs liked it higher in the Uinta Mountains and farther from the desert. He was away from the fires but had an escape plan just in case. His cell phone was charged, and he carried a portable charger in the camera bag. He looks across the water and speaks to himself.

"Some years ago, a seven-year-old girl drowned in Moon Lake, a small body of water high in the Utah Mountains. The lake is beautiful, here at mid-day, with the snow-capped peaks in the distance and the mix of pine and Aspen trees coming right up to the shore. No one knows who the girl was, but many have seen her since the water took her.

"It happens," Peter says, slowing down, "not at night as so many ghost stories wish you to believe, but rather now, as the sun beats down on the mirror of water and hikers or fishermen are more common. She walks up to you, cold despite the heat of day, her lips blue, her clothes dripping, and asks for help. You look around for her parents and when you turn around, the little girl has vanished."

He pauses, imagining such a girl walking up to him now when he hears crying behind him. He clicks the audio recorder attached to the camera on, but leaves the lens facing the lake. He picks up the narration, quieter than before, hoping the sobbing will be picked up. He doesn't turn around.

"Some people claim not to have seen the girl, but to only hear her cries during the day. They follow the wailing, calling out in return that help is on the way. All too often, a would-be rescuer is felled by a fallen tree or one of the rocky outcroppings hiding in the forest."

Stopping again, he waits. Yes, he can still hear the soft whimpering. Part of him wants to go toward it, to help where he can, but he knows he needs to stay put.

"At night, she doesn't cry. If you camp close enough to the waters of Moon Lake, you might hear her screaming, thrashing in the water, begging to be let go. Who... or what held her in the lake, dooming her to roam an otherwise perfect setting, we may never know."

Peter stops, thumb hovering over his remote, listening for the crying. It's gone. Without him speaking, everything is silent except the lapping of waves on the sparse beach. He hits the stop button, stands up, and the silence is broken.

***

"I am ... Ruin, and we are many," David said. The boy stated this as a matter of fact to the stranger in the black gloves. Peter stared at the boy, not exactly sure what to say. He didn't flinch, not wanting to reveal his surprise. He chose, instead, to roll with it.

"Hello, Ruin. Is this the Smith residence? I'm looking, maybe, for your mother. Madeleine's her name, right?"

"My mother is the pit and we shall all return to her womb." The boy's voice deepened, became quieter. "We all belong there."

"Does Mrs. Smith know you are speaking through her son, Ruin?"

"Do not speak my name lest the fire fall upon you."

"You don't like that, do you, Ruin?" Peter said, sensing an awkward weakness from whatever entity he spoke with. "Ruin? Do you know the Smiths?"

"I have been with the cow and the elder calf, and they stole me from me. What remains is here, in the young calf."

"May I speak with David?" Peter remained calm but saw the skin below David's eyes tremble, like something inside his sinuses wanted to cry but could not.

"Depart, warlock, with thine black hands intact. Return with your fleshmagic and see your hands severed." David—David's body, at least—stepped back into the house and slammed the door in Peter's face. Peter waited a moment before turning around to return to his car. He pulled his cellphone from his pocket and scrolled to the number for Grant Taysom, the LDS church archivist who'd sent him back to Blackhawk. Before he could dial, another voice, a kind but worn voice, interrupted him.

"We don't allow reporters, sir, so I would appreciate you leaving," Maddie Smith said. Looking up from the phone, Peter saw her and recoiled. He dropped the phone and it bounced off his foot. "I didn't mean to startle you, but you still need to leave," Maddie continued.

"Maddie...Knight?" The two words nearly didn't make it out of Peter's mouth. "Blackhawk High. We had Mr. Allred for Social Studies when I was a junior and you were a sophomore."

"There were a lot of people in that class," she said, keeping her distance and shifting her keys from between her fingers to a bunch in her fist. "How am I supposed to know you?"

"Mom! You went to high school with Peter Toombs? That's boss!" Brandon Smith came running up behind her, gently pushing her aside, and almost knocking Peter over. "I loved your show. I have all your books. At least, I think I do. Do you have a new one? Are you working on something now?"

"Slow down, champ," Peter said, keeping his "just friends" voice from his conversation with David. "Nothing new yet, but I'm working on something. Something you and your mom can help me with." He paused, picked up his phone, and spoke to Maddie. "If she's okay with it, that is."

Hesitation stopped Brandon cold. There was only one thing people wanted to talk to them about anymore. The cops, some lawyers, local reporters, and the Church—that had been the worst—they only wanted to talk about last summer.

"I don't think we can help you, Mr. Toombs," Maddie said. "Whatever it is you are looking for isn't here." She took a few steps forward, meaning to shove him out of the way if need be, but she froze at his next words.

"Grant Taysom sent me here. He was a friend of Rey Montoya. Here," Peter pushed the CALL button on his phone and reached it out toward her. "You can ask him yourself."

She did not want to take the phone because she knew it meant going over everything from last summer again, the parts she could remember and those she could not. The same went for Brandon, too. They'd barely survived. Only David seemed unharmed on the surface. Wiser and somewhat sullen, but unharmed at first glance. Maddie knew better. Her fingers brushed the tips of Peter's gloved fingers as she took the phone. As she put it to her ear, a familiar voice rang out of it.

"Peter? Did you meet Maddie yet?" Taysom said.

"Hello, Mr. Taysom. This is Maddie. Mr. Toombs is right here. He asked me to chat with you."

"Maddie, look, I know you won't be happy about this, but you should at least talk to him," Taysom told her through the phone. "Get him to tell his story and you might not have to say much at all. And make sure he pays for lunch."

She allowed a smile to touch her lips, and before she ended the call, she said, "Thank you, Grant. I will be in touch." She passed the phone back to Peter. "I have some things to put away. You may help Brandon bring the bags in the house. Afterward, I want you to stay outside and wait while I decided if we'll swap our tales."

Brandon and Peter made quick work of hauling the groceries inside. Each trip in, Peter searched for David, but didn't spot him. As they finished, he noticed Brandon's eyes glued to his gloves.

"You want to know why I'm wearing gloves in summer?" Peter asked the teen.

"Your Wikipedia page says you had some kind of accident in the mountains. Was it..." Brandon stifled a cry before completing his question. "Was it a fire?"

"There was a fire, but thankfully I was not in it." Peter could see the pain on the boy's face and knew he'd never get what he came for without giving up his own ghosts. "Maybe we can talk more about it."

"Outside now, Mr. Toombs," came Maddie's voice from the kitchen. "We won't keep you waiting long."

Peter left, closing the door softly behind him. Rubbing his hands together, he gazed at the summer sun and whispered to himself. "There's more here than I thought, Diana. I don't want to be here, but here I am."

***

The noise of the phone, the same one Peter had let Maddie speak to Taysom on, cuts through the forest quietude. After the sobbing and screaming, the phone's guitar solo ringing is welcome, but also distracting. He pulls it from its pocket and sees Maddie's home number on the screen. He also sees the bars flashing a low cell signal at him.

"Hey, Maddie," he starts. "Talk fast; the signal here sucks."

"Something... in town...and David...side...everywhere. Come...help... scared," he hears Maddie say, losing a word here and there. He gets the message before the call drops. Something is happening in town. Come back and help. We're scared. That middle part, though, something about David.

That scares him.

He doesn't like being scared, not like he used to, and so he hurries. He sets the equipment bag on his chair, unzipping it, first putting away the remote, then detaching the audio recorder and microphone from the camera. He hears a splash behind him as he finds the slots for the various equipment. Some lucky trout, happy Peter's left his pole behind. He hears another splash as he twists the camera off the tripod head. When the splashing stops and the crying begins again, he pivots toward the lake and sees her. The lost girl, blue-lipped and sopping wet, walks out of the lake, her hands held out before her, seeking rescue. He falls to his knees and the camera slips from his hands. He reaches out, gloveless today, praying this is not a dream, not like when he saw his never-born son. The girl steps closer, crying, never saying a word, her small shoulders shrugging. Her arms tremble and before her fingers can touch Peter's outstretched hands, her face changes. Her eyes widen and she says something but can't vocalize it. She points behind Peter and he turns his head to see what she sees.

He sees nothing. His world plummets into black.

***

The Church had been the worst about the possessions. Maddie and Brandon both testified to the reality of being overtaken by the demon who called itself Ruin. The only witness they could find to support them was Grant Taysom. With Montoya and Griffen both dead, Taysom was the only person who knew what had happened.

The threats became more extreme over time. Taysom's job was on the line at one point, but he'd gotten married and his wife was expecting. The disciplinary council had mercy on him for that.

Brandon, a deacon for only a year, cried when the council told him they could revoke his priesthood authority and he would never advance within the Church.

"I'll ordain him again myself," Maddie said, revealing for the first time that Montoya had ordained her in both the Aaronic and Melchizedek priesthoods, the two levels of Church power.

"Under whose authority did he do that?" The council chair Hyrum Wilkinson, a member of the Quorum of the Seventy, spat the question at her.

"Heavenly Father's," she replied without hesitation.

"It was a battlefield ordination in a moment of spiritual warfare," Taysom added.

"Were you party to this rogue ordination," Wilkinson asked Taysom.

"No, sir. I was informed of it after the fact. After Montoya died and while Sister Smith recounted the events leading to his death to me."

"Then no one else bore witness to this ordination?" another councilmember asked.

"The Lord granted Rey his authority and the insight to bless me with it," Maddie said. "If he hadn't, we wouldn't have been able to save my son. Rey died saving Brandon. What have you all sacrificed in your lives?"

The faces of four men flushed red, but one face remained pale. The councilmember at the end of the table had said nothing during the previous four meetings Maddie had been called into. Now, he spoke.

"Sister Smith, first let me introduce myself again. I am Benjamin Knost, bishop of the Spanish Fork Ninth Ward. I've stayed silent because, frankly, I couldn't believe we were even here. These meetings have tested my faith. I've read the scriptural accounts of demonic possession, and reviewed the accounts provided by Brother Taysom during these proceedings. I knew Rey Montoya to be a level-headed man of God. He was quicker to peace than anger. Reading his testimony regarding the events he and Bishop Griffen survived during their mission in Chile gave me a new insight into the man I knew." Knost took his glasses off and wiped his eyes. The other councilmembers shied away from him, but none interjected.

"And now we sit here, tasked to judge the worthiness in Christ of three individuals, two of whom have experienced

Hell on earth, and we are arguing about God-granted power and the existence of demons. Let me remind us all of some our own Articles of Faith. 'We believe that a man must be called of God, by prophecy, and by the laying on of hands by those who are in authority, to preach the Gospel and administer in the ordinances thereof.' Now I'm not here to say that the article states only a man, not a woman, may be granted priesthood authority. That is a topic beyond this one individual." Maddie watched the hunched shoulder of councilmembers and heard their muffled groans. Knost continued unabated. "The article states that a person must be called of God, first, and by prophecy, second. I would say this is exactly the situation Sister Smith found herself in. Third, Montoya, a member in good standing with the keys and authority granted to him in his position as President of the Nebo Stake, laid his hands upon Sister Smith and ordained her to the Priesthood. Perhaps it was just for that specific situation but let me take it one step further. Sister Smith is unequivocally the head of her household and while we, her brothers and sisters in the Church and in Christ, have a community responsibility to fill in where we can, she is the master of her household and by all rights should be able to perform as such."

Knost wiped his eyes once more, adjusted his tie, and bore in again as the councilmembers behind their table tried not to squirm. Maddie and Taysom sat at their own small table, each waiting to hear where Knost would go next.

"I will paraphrase a few more articles for you. We believe in all manner of Church positions. Preachers and pastors and so forth. We believe in the gifts of prophecy, revelation, and healing. We believe that God has more to reveal to us still.

"I believe what Sister Smith and Brother Taysom, and young Brother Smith who is hopefully comfortable at home now, have revealed to us. I believe many of us have become lost in our faith and no longer believe that Satan is real and among us today. I believe that we should let these people go home, maintaining their standing and all the gifts granted to them by Priesthood authority. We'd ask, Sister Smith, that you reign your Priesthood authority to your own home, but otherwise, I see no reason that we men should strip you of that gift.

"I say all these things with faith in and in the name of Jesus Christ. Amen."

The silence stretched out before the next councilmember voiced his agreement. The amens continued. At last, Wilkinson, adjourned the meeting, ready to report the disciplinary actions back to his Quorum of the Seventy

Not even Knost stuck around to shake hands with Taysom or Maddie.

***

She ended there, going over everything from visiting the now burnt to cinders house and touching the painting, to the letter she received two weeks after the council meeting, an official church document stating that no punitive action would be taken against her, Brandon, or Taysom.

"The next Sunday, I took the sacrament from Brandon with more joy than I had since I was a teenager," she said.

"I haven't taken the sacrament since I was not much older than he is," Peter said. "I drifted away a long time ago."

"I'm sorry about Diana. She was always someone I looked up to in school."

"I feel so old sometimes. She's been gone a long time and I'd lost her even before that. And I feel like such a jerk because I don't remember everyone from school. That's just not where my head was."

"But look at you now, Mr. TV. Brandon hasn't shut up about you. I mean, we all knew you were from here. Every now and again some fifth grader would come into school with one of your books. I don't think any of us ever thought you'd come back. And come back again, after that mess up in Bern."

"Somebody said, 'Horror is my business and business is good.' Living it, though, that's a different story." He slid a large manila envelope across the table to her. "It's all in there. Talking about it makes my skin crawl. I know that's not fair after getting you to tell me your tale, but it's faster this way. If you read it, I won't be able to gloss over details or avoid how much of an asshole I was."

She wanted to say she didn't think he was an asshole, but she still didn't really know who Peter Toombs was now. She didn't really know him in high school, either. Diana was the only one who knew and she wasn't available. She opened the envelope and pulled out the first page just enough to see the words:

CRY DOWN DARK

By

Peter Toombs

"Has anyone else seen this yet?" Maddie questioned, sliding the page back into the envelope.

"I workshopped a few chapters, but otherwise, no."

"You have a copy? This isn't the only one?"

"I always back up my files. You could barbecue that manuscript and I'd be fine." He waited for Maddie to get his literary joke but let it go. "The ending needs work, but I should have time to fix it later."

"It's short, is that normal?"

"It's the story I had to tell, so that's what counts."

"I'll read it tonight."

They finished their dinner surrounded by the chatter of other patrons and none of their own. Separately, they both wondered if this was a date, and without saying so concluded it was not. It was business, horrible business, but also good. Leaving it at that, Peter paid the check and walked Maddie to her car. He had someone else to see.

CHAPTER THREE

The sun glistens off of Moon Lake, its slivery roundness rippling, looking more like craters on the surface than a smooth mirror. No fish break the surface, the frogs croak to themselves, and the squirrels stay in the trees, waiting until dusk to drink from the lake. Then a rustling, a woman's laugh, a man's guffaw, the heavy steps of hikers emerging from the forest to the shore.

"Have you ever seen a lake like this?" Dale says to his newlywed wife Shirley. They are on their honeymoon, married in one of the many LDS temples in Utah three days prior. Instead of a cruise or a trip across the country, they decided to explore their home state more. Both had served missions abroad, and now wanted to reconnect with home and connect with each other without the headaches of too much travel.

"It's beautiful," Shirley says, setting her backpack on the ground, then stretching her arms above her. Dale admires her slim body and smiles are her temple garments peek out of the short sleeves of her shirt. "Can we set up camp here?"

"Yeah, I have the permit, we just have to find a clear spot."

"Looks like we aren't alone, though," Shirley says, disappointed. She's enjoyed her husband alone, as any new bride would, and had hoped for more of that most special time alone with him. "What's that?"

They walk closer to the shore and the black object poking out of the ground. Sand has blown against it, a few leaves and pine needles, too. Scratches on the dark metal where an animal tested its worthiness as food and found it lacking.

"It's a camera tripod," Dale said, grasping it and pulling it up out of the sand. "A nice one, too."

"Who would leave it behind? And here," Shirley says, squatting down, brushing away debris to uncover a camera, "is the camera that goes with it. I don't like this, Dale."

A shushing rises between them and they face each other. "What?" they say, followed by, "Jinx. You owe me a Sprite." They laugh as only young couples laugh and the shushing returns.

"That wasn't me," Shirley says.

"Me, neither," says Dale.

"Then who..." Shirley starts, taking a few steps backward before tripping over an unseen lump. "Ow!"

Dale springs to his wife. "You okay?" he asks, carefully holding her hands. He pulls her to her knees, then joins her there. Together, they dig out the cause of Shirley's plummet: a bag. Empty candy bar wrappers, a shredded bag of sunflower seeds, and cans of soda—some smashed for recycling and others punctured on the sides—are in the bag. So is a wallet. Shirley hands it to Dale.

"The license says 'Peter Toombs.' Isn't that that TV guy?" Dale says.

"Where is he now? This stuff's been here awhile," Shirley says, a shiver of fear running over her, cooling her sweaty body in an unpleasant manner.

"I don't know, but I don't like it." Dale takes Shirley's hand and together they stand. "We should call someone.

Let's find a good spot to sit and I'll try to get a signal. If I can't, we'll hike back down to the ranger station."

***

Maddie couldn't stop reading Peter's manuscript. She hated horror novels and movies—even more since last summer—and had avoided his other books. She didn't let Brandon watch either of Peter's TV shows, despite Peter's hometown boy made good status. But here she was, turning the final pages, seeing him in her mind, his glossy black gloves in front of his chest, telling an audience that they have no idea what real horrors are in the world. She hadn't known, not really, and before reading this she would have assumed Peter to be a hack that didn't know, either. Instead, she believed every word he wrote. Even the shitty ending.

She hadn't realized she'd been crying until David came into her room, asking for a drink of water. "You can get your own water, honey," she said.

"I need you to," David said, his voice sounding as if he were still asleep.

"Okay, come on." They walked together to the kitchen. All three of them were still getting used to the new house. It was smaller, but everyone had their own room and Maddie had her own bathroom. "You want tap water or from the fridge, dude?"

"Either, but I need you to bless it," David said.

"What, honey? You need me to say a prayer? You sure you're okay?"

"Not a prayer, a blessing," David said, his voice still sleep-tinged but becoming more deliberate. "Like sacrament water."

"I can't do that, honey."

"Yes, you can." His voice had now lost all sense of tiredness, although his face in the low light of night, still appeared slack. "Do the blessing, with your authority, and let me drink."

She couldn't remember the sacrament prayers, hadn't needed to rehearse them as the young men do. She did her best, shaking with worry, spilling some of the water on her arm. "Oh, Lord. Bless this water in remembrance of the blood you shed for us. In Jesus name, amen." As she finished, David snatched the glass from her hand.

"Remember this?" he said. He held the clear glass from the bottom, allowing Maddie to see the liquid thicken and darken. "Remember the water you tasted that first day we met? Like blood and ash?" Small flames circled the opening and the crimson fluid began to boil. David tipped the glass to his lips and guzzled the heated contents without stopping. After swallowing it all, he spoke again. "We remember."

He dropped the glass—*thank you, Jesus, that it did not shatter*, Maddie thought—and walked back to his bedroom. Maddie followed seconds later, peeking into David's room only to see him on his side, fast asleep as if he'd not moved since going to bed.

She did not see the dream-David, the thirsty one, his lips stained red, leering at her from beneath the bed.

*****

Taysom wanted to be done with it. The disciplinary council came so soon after his wedding. Amy, his now pregnant wife, even told him not to take the call from a name he recognized but didn't know.

"It sounds like trouble," she'd said after they listened to the voicemail together. "Don't get involved."

"I won't," he said and that was the first lie he'd told her.

He called Peter from his office that Monday. Peter had known just the right questions to ask and Taysom gave him all the information he wanted, including Maddie Smith's phone number and new address. He'd call Maddie next, to warn her, to apologize to her. To tell her she didn't have to talk to Peter if she didn't want to. Then another call came, a member of the Quorum of the Twelve needed archives related to the Church's early mission work in England for his General Conference talk. Getting to work with one of the Church's apostles was a privilege and Taysom dove right into that work. He didn't speak to Maddie again until Peter was at her front doorstep.

The fires and the earthquakes came later. In between, Taysom lost everything that mattered.

***

A second copy of the manuscript in an identical envelope sat on the passenger seat of Peter's Mustang. A pamphlet for the new electric Mustang poked out from beneath the envelope. He'd been thinking of upgrading, but Marla had driven to Bern twice and survived. He managed to avoid the rash of dents and dings that plague most cars in L.A. and the maniacs on the stretch of Interstate 15 from Ogden to Las Vegas. If there wasn't construction, there was traffic, but mostly there was both.

The drive ahead wouldn't take long. Debbie Ward might not even be home. He thought about calling her first, telling her he was in town, preventing an awkward meeting at the park or during lunch at Walt's. Ten years had passed since he got her away from those nutjobs in Bern. They'd tried to drive him crazy, making him believe they were bringing

Debbie's older sister Diana back from the dead. Even now, he wasn't entirely sure what they had planned for Debbie, but he knew it wouldn't have been good. He'd broken both his arms during the rescue. The gloves he wore covered the scars from various surgeries that gave him back the use of his hands.

Hands he could have used to dial Debbie's number...if he'd known it.

Her address, though, that he knew. He'd sent flowers when Mr. Ward passed five years ago and again only a year before when Mrs. Ward died. Both times, he'd received delivery confirmation. The Wards home near the mouth of Blackhawk Canyon had once been like a second home to him, if only for a little while. He could drive there without looking.

Or he could turn the other way. Get back on the freeway for a few miles, hit another canyon road and be in Bern before KSL News signed off with an editorial.

Third time's a charm, right? he thought, drumming his fingers on the steering wheel to Gun N' Roses. *Screw it. Just go back to your hotel. Go to sleep and maybe tomorrow you can drive up there. It'll be almost dark and you don't want to do that to yourself. Not in the dark.*

He was right, on all counts. A third trip to Bern would be a charm, just not at night. The Ward home—not the one near the canyon in Blackhawk but the one on hill in Bern, the one he'd owned for a year—was a bed & breakfast now and tourism in the imitation Swiss village had boomed. He'd sold cheap and never looked back.

Who are you kidding? You look back all the time. What do you think that book is, except a look back?

But he'd needed to write it, even if he had to fudge a few things to pass it off as fiction. Ten years he plugged away at it. Wild spurts in which the words—and tears—flowed in between years of not touching it while he worked on other projects. Nobody would believe it anyway, if he'd written it to be a memoir. A new Peter Toombs novel, though? His agent Leslie had been asking for a new manuscript forever. So there it was: two printouts and its digital life on his laptop.

The Mustang sat in neutral still, rumbling as Peter remained indecisive. He stared out the window, watching seagulls battle over someone's leftovers that had been dropped in the parking lot.

Okay, let's go.

"Where?" he answered himself aloud.

Before an answer came, his phone rang. Not looking, he tapped the green button to answer it. "Toombs," he said. "What's up?"

"It's Grant. Grant Taysom. You have a minute?"

"I do."

"I hope Mrs. Smith is doing well. She didn't sound too pleased that I'd sent you there."

"She's coming around. I got a short version of her story and I don't blame her for being standoffish. We all have things we don't like to discuss." Peter ran his hand over the envelope, remembering how he crawled through glass shards after Ben Hill, the bookseller of Bern, had been killed inside his own store.

"Yeah, she's burnt out on repeating it over and over. I don't know if you'll get what you are after, but two good men lost their lives helping her and her boys." Taysom shuffled some papers before continuing. "In case it doesn't work out with Maddie, I dug up some other stuff that might interest you. Cult activity up in the mountains, a haunted lake, and even a couple creepy stories from right there in Blackhawk."

Cult activity in the mountains nearly sent the whole thing spiraling away from Peter, but a lake with a ghost sounded good, and if he could add some flavor with other paranormal events here, well, that would just make Maddie's story that much deeper and...

Enticing to viewers. You are still such a jerk.

"Thanks, Grant. Give me the gist and I'll get back to you. Skip the cults, though. I don't want to get into any of the Church offshoots."

"Emailing you now. Might be a good time of year to get up to Moon Lake, you know. The hiking and camping are good, but once August hits, it'll be too hot to do anything, even at that elevation."

"Thanks for the tips. And hey, don't worry about Maddie. She's a tough one."

"That is an understatement. Let me know if you need anything else." Taysom hung up and Peter watched for the email notification on his phone. The red 1 popped up and Peter verified that it was from Taysom. Then he put the phone on top of the envelope, put the Mustang in gear, and rolled out of the lot.

***

Brandon tossed and turned, threw his covers onto the floor, and tried to sleep without them. The nightmares always came right when he'd least expected them. But tonight there were no nightmares, no dreams at all, because he hadn't been able to rest. If he opened his eyes, he would be able to see his copies of *Graveyard Paradise* comics and the hardbacks of *Scream Queen* and *Takes My Life* that he'd bought during a library sale and were now signed by Peter Toombs.

Maddie had come home from dinner with an envelope and a smile. Brandon was happy to see her smile, but the envelope had caught his eye. "What's that?" he asked his mom.

"It's Mr. Toombs' newest book. Or manuscript, I guess. It's not a real book until it's published," she said.

"Whoa, Mom. He gave you an unpublished manuscript? Can I see it? What's it called? Please, can I see it?"

"Maybe later. I'm supposed to read it. I told him what happened to us—"

"Oh, geez, Mom. Why? You know what he writes and what his shows are about? I don't want to be in a book or on TV about that."

"And he gave me this. He says it's his story about something that happened to him. It's supposed to make me—I suppose us—feel better about talking to him."

"Then I should get to read it, too. Will you ask him?"

"I will read it first and if it's something I think you should be allowed to read, then I will ask. That good?"

"Yeah, I suppose."

For an hour, Brandon watched his mother read, her pace not fast enough for him. With every turn of the page, he had another question. He remained silent. Maddie remained silent. They could both hear David playing with his handheld video games down the hall.

Finally, Maddie spoke. "You need to go to bed. I should be done in the morning and we'll call Mr. Toombs."

"Yes! Thank you so much, Mom. Riley will be so freaking jealous," Brandon said. "His mom lets him watch *Graveyard Paradise*, you know? When can I?"

"When they make a PG-13 version. Those comics are bad enough. You can't even take them to school without Mr. Keene taking them away."

"Mr. Keene has a Rob Zombie tattoo. Nick Barker says he saw it one day at the water park. It's on his shoulder where no one sees it during the day."

"Nick Barker's glasses fog up when he sweats a little. I don't believe he'd know a Rob Zombie tattoo from some fake Cracker Jack tattoo. Now go to bed."

"Mom..."

"What, Brandon? I know it's still summer but you need to go to bed."

"Is Mr. Toombs going to help us with David?"

She set the stack of papers down, checking to make sure none slipped out of order, then held her hands out to her oldest son. Brandon placed his hands in hers and waited.

"Dear Heavenly Father," Maddie began her prayer. "Thou hast sent us helpers when we needed them and in thine own time. We don't yet know if Mr. Toombs, Peter, is a helper or just another lookie-loo. We don't know if Thou hast sent him or if he comes from the Adversary. We do know that our faith in Thy plan is unwavering, even when it is not clear to us. Help us to see and know the helpers. This we pray in the name of Jesus Christ. Amen."

"Amen." Brandon felt a strength in his mother that had not been there before last summer. Before a demon calling itself Ruin had a turn inside each of them. He didn't feel as strong as her felt she was. He knew, though, that it would take more than this new strength in Maddie to help his little brother. Maybe Peter Toombs had it, too. Maybe it was in that new book, still just in printer paper and on the floor of their living room. He'd have to wait to find out.

"I love you, Mom," he said, hugging her like he was a toddler.

"I love you, Brandon. Now off to bed."

***

Shirley and Dale take the camera and the wallet but leave the tripod and the bag near Moon Lake. Hiking back toward the ranger station, Dale still attempting to get a call through, they do not see the little drowned girl trying to point in another direction. They do not see the trampled undergrowth, matted down from Peter's unconscious body being drug through the forest and away from the lake. They do not hear the thump of Peter's body hitting the bed of a truck nor the slam of the truck's door as the truck had left hours before Dale and Shirley reached the lakeshore.

They do not see Peter's head bumping against the truck bed he is being driven away from the lake, each thud deepening the throb of pain that will greet Peter when he awakens.

Peter does not see where he is being taken. He does not see the man at the steering wheel of the truck, nor the intermittent shafts of sunlight breaking through the trees as he is being driven away from the drowned girl and his equipment. The next thing he sees, he will wish he hadn't.

CHAPTER FOUR

"A hundred years ago, this area near Blackhawk, Utah, was mostly willow trees. The metropolitan sprawl that now makes the once-small town feel more like a small city seemed miles away in 1920. One day that winter, two boys found a man hanged in the willows. They ran, screaming down the train tracks, until they found Doug Stanley, a local merchant's son. They told Mr. Stanley what they'd seen. Stanley and another man drove his car as near to where the boys directed them as they could."

Peter walked in front of the camera, holding a necktie in his hands. Not taking his eyes off the camera's red "record" light, he sat down on a weathered stump and continued narrating.

"Doug Stanley walked into a portrait of death unlike any he had expected. A young man sat hunched over on this very stump, his necktie a noose tied to a low willow limb. Doug verified that the man was indeed dead and undid the noose.

"An advertisement seeking the identification of the man went out across the country and soon reached the man's parents in Nebraska. But after claiming and burying the body, they received a phone call on Christmas Day."

Peter stood and placed the tie around his neck, cinching it up, turning his collar back down over it. "The call was from their son." He let the sentence linger, an effect he knew could be done in editing, but that he enjoyed capturing on camera himself. "Who these grieving parents buried in their son's grave is still a mystery. Blackhawk, this small Mormon town, has more mysteries than you'd ever imagine. Each is a tale of grief and sadness.

"Welcome to the Lamentations of Blackhawk."

***

"You're kidding me," Peter said to Taysom the day after having dinner with Maddie. "That's great!"

"Didn't you know any of this?" Taysom said, a mildly perplexed look crossing his face. "I mean, you grew up there."

"You know how it is. No one tells you anything other than to go to church, say your prayers, don't have sex, and families can be together forever. Of course I don't know any of this." Peter shuffles through the files Taysom brought him: horse thieves, uncouth familial relations, murders, murders, murders, and a wild story about one of his own relatives.

"Elisha Toombs would have been my great-great grand uncle, if my math is right. The Toombs family hasn't exactly been model Mormons. I'm sure someone's done the genealogy, but I never really paid attention to it. How'd you find these letters?" Peter pulls a handful of pages to the top, photocopies of yellowing letters signed by Elder Elisha Toombs, sent from his mission in England.

"One of the Twelve requested documents related to the British missions and I came across these. The originals were carefully sealed and I doubt anyone has looked at them since they were filed away. The Church is meticulous about the archives and the last date on these is 1901 but the signature is smudged. I can't make out who was the last person to hold them."

"This sounds a lot like what Maddie says happened to her."

"Wait. What *she says* happened to her?" Taysom leans in and slaps a hand down over the files. "You don't believe her?"

"I just met her. Well, met her now. We had high school classes together, but I don't remember much from those days. She certainly believes what she says. And that's something."

"Two good men—and three scumbags—died. There was a body in that cellar. Rey Montoya wouldn't have lied to me with a gun to his head."

"But he never told you about Chile? Not before all this?"

"That's not lying. It's not something that just comes up."

"'Hey, have you ever performed an exorcism? Comes up all the time with people I know,' Peter said, then laughed. He didn't want Taysom angry at him. Based on what Taysom had just shown him, Peter needed this man more than ever. "I get asked that at least once a week. Now I'll just tell Joe Bob the next time he asks that I don't know what he's talking about, but I have dispossessed a few demons."

Taysom looked like he was going to continue to be offended. Instead he leaned back in his own chair. "He was here, you know. When they shot that miniseries back in the '90s. I wasn't even born yet."

"I was a teen. I wanted to be there," Peter said. Memories threatened to flood back. Memories from before he'd even met Diana Ward. The frustrated and angry Peter Toombs that he'd fought hard to put away.

"You're here now. Maddie's story is true. If you are planning to use it for a show, that's up to her. But since you are here, you might as well not waste your time."

"Thank you for this. The old-timers are going to be pissed. Some of the young ones, too, might already be angry."

"There aren't that many old-timers left to be mad."

Before meeting with Taysom—and the goldmine of spooky stories Taysom had brought with him—Peter had spent the day walking around Blackhawk. The manuscript he meant for Debbie sat on the passenger seat where he'd left it the night before and he didn't drive to Bern, either. He'd get to both of those things but after dinner with Maddie, he decided to drive to the house that had started her troubles.

He parked across the street. Crumbling black piles still stood where some of the brickwork had once been. The porch columns were gone, but he could picture the home that had once stood there. He had to dig into his but could remember riding his bike down this street during the summer and passing the house, one of a number of sandstone Victorians in Blackhawk. His mother had once told him that the founders of Blackhawk, sent down by Brigham Young himself, had fancied themselves fancier than they were.

Fancied themselves fancy was a phrase he thought captured Blackhawk perfectly. With its "Anytown, USA" Main Street that had caught the eyes of Hollywood even when he was a kid and its now lost separation from the sprawl of Utah's urbanization, Blackhawk had felt otherworldly to Peter, but not in the way he wished it had. There was an allure to a town that didn't have a McDonald's until the mid-1980s or a big box department store until the late 2000s. Blackhawk had been a place that had everything you needed: a couple decent restaurants, its own greasespot diners, great Little League baseball during the summer, and a perfect— as far as Peter was concerned—single-screen movie theater. Trips to the mall in Orem were saved for Back to School and

Christmas shopping, and the most devout members of the Church would go to the temple in Provo or Manti.

Looking for any neighbors, Peter got out of his car and watched to the patch of scorched earth that had almost claimed Brandon Smith's life and did take the lives of Blaine Griffen and the three men who were now assumed to have murdered and buried Samantha Robinson in the cellar floor.

The smell of smoke lingered throughout the lot, but nothing seemed to still be burning all these months later. Kicking at a lump of debris, Peter knocked a partial brick into the hole that went into what had been the cellar. *They should rope this off*, he thought. *Some stupid kid could come by and fall in.*

Some stupid kid, a teen, drove by and honked when passing Peter. Indecipherable expletives were shouted, but the honk had pulled Peter out of his revery. He knelt, pulling a plastic baggie out of his pocket. He scooped ash into the baggie and twisted it closed.

The water tasted like ashes, all burnt and gritty. It was red so I thought at first it should have tasted like copper—like blood. But it didn't; it tasted like ash.

Maddie had told him everything she could remember: going into the house, going upstairs and downstairs. Waking up in filth at her old house. Fighting the demon Ruin in the cemetery with Rey Montoya. She talked less about the reporters and the strange looks she got at work that school year. The spots vacated by students whose parents requested a teacher change were filled by other kids of other parents who hadn't heard any of the rumors or didn't care about them. She talked about the last meeting in front of the church disciplinary board.

But he knew there was something missing: she did not talk about David.

She spoke about Brandon and his recovery, how she'd fear he'd have PTSD for the rest of his life. Not a word of her younger son. The one who told Peter that the demon who'd taken over first Maddie and then Brandon was now inside him.

He didn't think Maddie would be able to go over the whole ordeal again. Putting the baggie of ashes in his jacket pocket, he felt assured that she would never have to. The digital recorder had come in handy more than once and he thought that after this he would grant it a well-earned retirement.

He spun away from the hole in the ground, its own portal to a mini-Hell, and took a few steps toward his car. Just as he placed a foot on the road, the truck that had driven by with its unrecognizable taunts gunned forward with its lights off and nearly ran him over. Instead, the truck stopped, its rolled-down driver's window right in front of Peter. The interior was still dark, but the face inside looked vaguely familiar.

"My uncle died because of you, you fuck," came a young but determined voice. "You got this town's best cop killed for nothing."

"Raines?" Peter said, unsure of himself for the first time in ... days.

"Yeah. Raines. Wally Raines is my name and I want you out of here. I might not tell the rest of the police that you're snooping around at another crime scene, but I just might." Raines spat out the window, somehow missing Peter. The truck's headlights came on and Peter wisely stepped back, not wanting the back tires to finish the job the front tires left incomplete.

Taking deep breaths and watching to make sure Wally Raines rolled on down the road, Peter recalled how welcome the residents had made him feel in Bern. He remembered Sergeant Raines being stern and brave, during the brief time he'd known the officer. He didn't remember his first name, and that made him sad for a moment. Every town had a memorial to the fallen and tomorrow he'd check it out and find Sergeant Raines' first name.

Wally Raines, and anyone else who wanted to drive him out of town, could go fuck themselves. That was, now, just Peter's style.

Strolling through town the next morning, his meeting with Taysom hours away, Peter took in all that he had missed. No one took more than a casual glance at him as he leaned on the small counter, ordering an Iron Port from the Daley Freez, or as he ambled up Main Street, passing storefronts that weren't the same as when he was a kid. Part of him expected them to be the same, but he knew that wasn't realistic. Even the bakery famous for its alligator jaws—a triangular doughnut cut in half and filled with crème—was a cellphone repair shop now. Closer to the park, a few things hadn't changed. The butcher shop, the locksmith, and the mechanic shop where his mom always took her car for its annual inspection were still there.

The mechanic was out of business, but it was still there.

At the park, Peter laid down on a large patch of grass where there had been a pool when he was a kid. Unless you knew it had been there, you'd never know it was anything other than the grassiest part of the park. Soon, just after school started for the year, the park would be full of people like him. People coming back to Blackhawk and telling tales of when they grew up. When they'd burn their butts on the metal slides that had been replaced years ago, or how they'd always have to get out of the pool once an hour to take a break. Everyone sitting on the edges, kicking water as hard as they could for five minutes before the lifeguards whistled their permission to re-enter the water.

All of that was before the fires and earthquakes, though. At this moment, even Peter thought he could stay here again. He could be home.

He remembered sitting on the swings and reading bad poetry to Diana: the worst kind of heartfelt teenage boy with a passion for theater poetry. His verse had leaned more toward Poe even then than Shakespearian sonnets. Diana would laugh more often than not. Any reaction was better than nothing, he remembered thinking. He closed his eyes against the sun and decided to lay there until someone came along to make him move.

Memorial Park began to fill with people and noise. Before long, Peter heard a gruff voice blast out from an amplifier. "We are The Atomic Blue, we're from Blackhawk, and we are here to melt your faces off!" The singer launched into an impressive cover of Black Sabbath's "Heaven or Hell."

It's not so black and white, Peter thought. *Sometimes we're in heaven and hell. I might have to go check out this band.*

After a couple more quality cover songs and before Peter decided to get up and see the band, the wet tongue of a dog made him move. Peter sat up faster when he heard the dog's owner call it. "Bertrand! Down," Debbie Ward called to the golden retriever slathering over Peter's face.

Peter laughed a pure laughter that he'd almost forgotten he had inside him. He patted Bertrand's yellow fur as he hoisted himself up to his knees. Once the laughter and the slobbering subsided, Peter said hello.

"I thought that was you," Debbie said. "Your hair is still hard to miss."

Running his hands through his hair felt odd. Not just because of the saliva-matted portions but because he'd forgotten to put his gloves on. "It's not quite as bright as it used to be. I went and got old."

"We all are," Debbie said, attaching a leash to Bertrand's collar. "I heard you were in town. How long you here?"

"I'm not sure. I thought just a few days, but it might be more. I'm on to something that could be a goof or could be big for me." He stood and put his hands in his pockets. He'd left his gloves in the car and he felt embarrassment creeping up from his fingertips and into the scars that wound their way across his forearms.

"Something big here? For you? The biggest thing you'll get here is the double bacon deluxe at Walt's and maybe a few sideways glances. The library even replaced that shelf of your stuff with Brandon Sanderson novels. If you are here to act famous, you should just move along back to California or wherever to live now."

"Debbie, look," he started, stunned at the hostile tone coming from her. "I'm not here to bother you or your family. I heard about something that happened here last year and I decided to check it out. That's all." His mind turned toward the manuscript in his car and he thanked whatever god watched over him that he didn't go to Debbie's house last night. He'd just have to ask forgiveness later instead of permission now.

"Nothing ever happens here. They haven't even finished the memorial for that cop or gotten passed planning another one for..." She pulled Bertrand closer to her while the large dog set and reset its paws, ready to run and lick the next face it could get to. "That's why you're here, isn't it? That fire and the men who died... the body they found. You just can't leave people be, can you?"

"I guess not. Once a decade or so, I get pretty nosy."

"You could have been a little nosier, you know," Debbie said, softening her attack voice for a moment. "We all could have helped each other more."

"I know, I just—"

"Just shut up. I get it. I'm glad you sold the house."

"They did it up really nice, I heard." They both stood now, Bertrand chomping his jaws and twitching at something only dogs see.

"Jay and I stayed up there. It was weird. No one knew who we were—who I was. It felt good not to be gawked at. The store there still has all your books. The owner's niece took it over." Debbie gazed downward at her dog, at the grass, then back at Peter. "You have anything new coming out?"

***

His head is still, no longer bumping against the metal of a truck bed. The throbbing persists, pulsing from the base of his skull up over the rest of his head and into his eyes. The pounding radiates through his collarbones and along his shoulders, spiking down his arms, hitting all the places that once had metal pins holding him together.

He tries to speak, but something soft and filthy prevents his tongue from moving. Against the pain, he opens his eyes, seeing nothing but the darkness. A shuffling behind him causes his head to try and follow the sound, to place it, but his motion is limited by the aching and the covering over his head.

"I had friends up in Bern. I doubt you knew that." The voice is familiar but Peter can't place it. I was just a kid when you got Uncle James killed there. People knew him, too, but they couldn't stop it. He wouldn't have been there if it wasn't for you."

Peter hears another shuffling, faster this time, then feels a hard sole kick his upper thigh. The new agony joins the former somewhere along his spine. Another kick and Peter cries out against the gag in his mouth. He can feel tears running down his face, pooling below his chin where the hood is pulled tight. A few gasps and he believes he might suffocate without seeing his abductor.

"Can't breathe, can you?" the voice asks with the authority of one who knows the answer. "That sock in your mouth came right off my foot yesterday. My foot smell taste good, you bastard?" A punch connects high on Peter's shoulder and the sock slips farther into his mouth. He isn't choking yet, but soon, he knows. And if he does, he won't choke for long.

"I've been following you since I saw you out at that house." A stomp on Peter's left foot. "Just waiting for you to take off alone where people wouldn't expect you back." Now the right foot, ensuring that no place on Peter's body was pain free. A slap across the face and—*gah*—and audible choking noise from behind the hood. "I knew you'd wander away eventually."

Feeling nothing but suffering, Peter tries to focus. If these are his last breaths, he would take them without a sweaty piece of footwear in his mouth. He dips his head forward and can feel one end of the sock rub against the hood. He turns his head, looking as if he is shaking cobwebs from his brain. Then he finds it: the place where the hood is cinched tight. He won't be able to loosen the hood, he accepts that. But he can get his tongue behind the sock and push it against the solidity of the knob holding it in place. His torturer has let him be just long enough to proceed before Peter hears another sound, worse than the shuffling that came before the kicks.

Snick! The sharp retort of a large-bladed pocketknife being flicked open. *Snap!* The *snick* and *snap* repeats and just as Peter spits the sock out of his mouth, he hears a *snick* but no *snap*.

"When I was eight, Uncle James took me to Lagoon," the still unseen voice said. "I was tall for my age, so I could ride almost everything. Then he followed your stupid ass up in the mountains not even two months later. He took me to the rides because my daddy'd lost his job and even on good days he could be punchy. Uncle James was the only one who tried to keep me safe."

"Wally," Peter croaks with one of his first breaths. "Your uncle was just doing his job. Those folks in Bern were crazy."

Peter feels the *woosh* of air and the opening of his shirt but nothing else. The knife misses his chest.

"Those people in Bern, the ones who got out of the cemetery, found me and made me a new family," Wally screams. Peter senses Wally's arm coming down and braces for the stab. Wally misses again, slicing through the side of Peter's pants, but not penetrating the muscle with the blade. The sharp blade slivers off a few layers of skin, immediately soaking Peter's thigh in blood. He reaches for the wound, but his hands are bound. With his mouth open in a scream, the sock he worked so hard to dislodge nearly falls back into place. His howls do not stop Wally's monologue and so he prepares for another jab, one that will find its target.

"Those good people found me and took me in. They raised me and told me what happened. The plans they had for Bern and the future. But you fucked up their lives over your dead girlfriend. They had to settle for being a normal dipshit tourist town instead of a new capital." Wally breathes and Peter can hear anger and adrenaline in the air Wally pulls.

Peter waits. He breathes the best he can with a sack over his head. His thigh throbs and bleeds, the oozing blood coating the space between his skin and the fabric of his pants.

And then the breathing stops. Peter no longer hears Wally Raines. He hears a *clunk*, the knife hitting the floor. He hears scraping, like a body being dragged on hardwood.

He hears a soft weeping that is both far away and inside his head.

Sensing no weight or closeness of another body, the hood over Peter's head is loosened. He sits, waiting to see if the hood will come off on its own. It does not. His hands, which had been bound behind him, swing freely to his sides and despite the surging agony in them, he raises them to his neck, loosens the hood more, and pulls the black hood from off his head. The sock falls to floor. With the hood off, his hands go to his thigh. He doesn't look, just applies pressure. He blinks once, twice, and again before seeing Wally's body, propped up against the far wall of the room they are in, the knife poking out from his chest.

A sigh of relief begins in his lungs but dies as a shadow falls over Wally's body. The shadow hovers over the knife and the hole in Wally's chest. Silently, it soaks the blood pouring from the wound into itself and becomes more solid. An appendage, not quite a hand, reaches for the knife and pulls, but the knife doesn't budge. A second appendage, both looking more like tentacles than arms, joins the first, wrapping around the handle of the knife.

Rather than pulling, the dark tentacles lift. They hoist Wally's body into the air, still holding nothing but the knife. The corpse is dragged through the air and dumped at Peter's feet, facedown. A thunderclap of air turns the body over and the knife springs out of its chest like the first kernel of popcorn in a stir-fryer. Peter attempts to push himself back to avoid the knife's downward trajectory, but one shadow arm catches the blade. Two new tentacles grow from the mass and engulf the corpse until it disappears from Peter's sight.

Slowly, the entire shadow leaks through the cracks in the floor, leaving nothing behind except the clean and closed knife, now laying at Peter's foot, a few inches away from the pool of blood from his wounded thigh.

CHAPTER FIVE

"I don't want to do that."

You must. We must. You want to be strong.

"No. I want to be asleep."

No sleep, child. First do.

"I don't want to scare her like that."

You must, or...

Visions of collapsing buildings, animals running from flames, his mother screaming his name assaulted David's mind. He cried, hoping no one heard. The voice did not relent. A deer caught on fire, a golden statue crumbled, Maddie fell to her knees, bleeding from her pores.

You must

"Okay, just stop."

***

Even with a shifting student body, school started as regularly as it could. Maddie saw familiar faces among her kids, meaning she'd their older siblings in class at some point during her career at Erickson Elementary, one of the ever-growing number of grade schools serving Blackhawk. She did her best to ignore the sideways glances and chatter and focus on her students. David was down the hall in fifth grade and Brandon was across town at the middle school. They would survive another year and keep moving forward.

The early October night when David showed Maddie his trick with the glass of water threatened to bring everything crashing back down. She's survived church discipline, had been faithfully partaking of the sacrament, and prayed every morning. She could hear Brandon's nightly prayers and David's mumbles that she assumed were prayers. She was still learning to trust her new bishop, another old man who not only didn't understand women, but also preferred to embrace an older school brand of the Church of Jesus Christ of Latter-Day Saints. Even when the church changed, he didn't.

So Maddie had no one to turn to.

After seeing David back to bed, Maddie went to her room and prayed through tears.

David's tricks were few and far between, until Peter Toombs showed up at their house. She'd convinced herself that she'd been dreaming when David predicted little league scores, playground injuries, car accidents. And then nothing for most of the summer.

And then Peter Toombs, in his black gloves and thinking he knew everything, showed up. And now, as wildfires raged around them and aftershocks trembled over the state, the one person she tried to call wouldn't answer.

***

Toombs showed up just after Pioneer Day in late July. The first August wildfire started small and was snuffed out in less than a day. Forty-eight hours later, the next fire started, again small, but more persistent. It started higher in the mountains, making it harder for firefighters to reach. So they watched and prepared, ready to stamp it out as they could.

Then it jumped, raged down the canyon toward Blackhawk, obliterating homes in the small town of Elk Ridge before seeming to stop right at the city limits.

The trajectory of Taysom's downfall started before Toombs showed up in Blackhawk. The first fire started when he returned Toombs' phone calls, but he snuffed out the concerns of his wife, saying it was nothing, and would go away. Then Toombs really did come to Blackhawk, and Taysom had found some of the town's secrets.

And shared them with Toombs. Perhaps if he'd kept them to himself, he'd be fine. But his wife found the story of the Blackhawk horse thieves and that was the real beginning of the end.

"Is this stuff true," Lisa asked him, holding up a folder marked **HORSE THIEVES** on the front. It wasn't people stealing horses that bothered her.

"Yeah, near as I can tell. A mother and son set of thieves who happened to be closer to each other than the community thought they should be."

"That's one way to put it. You should just let this go, whatever it is. I don't like you reading about mobs killing people, even if they were... doing that."

"There was incest in the Bible, you know."

"Yeah, I know. I hear all the rumors, the old ones and the new ones. And I think you should just leave it alone."

"I will. Once I get this stuff to that Toombs guy, I'm out."

And that was another lie.

***

For Brandon, the school year and the ensuing summer went like a blur. He studied harder than ever, devoted himself to the weekly Young Men's meetings, and volunteered to be a den chief for the Cub Scouts. They had plenty of volunteers that year and, being so busy, he didn't give it another thought. He was too young to get a job, and so he read more. He devoured the novels and graphic novels written by Peter Toombs after learning he was from Blackhawk. He read Utah history and LDS history. It was not unusual to see him carrying a large hardback horror novel and his Book of Mormon together. His friends goaded him about it, saying he should stick to Tolkien, Sanderson, or Terry Brooks. His friends, that is, except Riley. Riley stayed more dedicated to church than anyone else Brandon knew. And yeah, he'd fibbed about Riley watching *Graveyard Paradise*. Even if his parents had let him watch the gore-filled series, he wouldn't have.

To Brandon, the violence in the horror novels he read and the violence—wars, rapes, slaughters beyond counting—in the scriptures served to show different versions of the battles between good and evil. He knew that on Earth, good didn't always win.

So as David convulsed on the living room floor and the house shook, while the trumpets of the Angel Moroni fell, Brandon knew he could talk to Heavenly Father later. First, they had to call Peter.

He watched Maddie dial as he sat next to his brother. He knew what his brother was going through, had seen some of the signs himself but ignored them. He wished he hadn't.

"Pick up, Peter," Maddie said. "Where are you?"

"By the shore of the moon," David whispered. "One of many has him now."

"Mom! Did you hear that?" Brandon shouted.

"Just a second, let me leave a message." Maddie said.

"MOM! David thinks someone has Mr. Toombs."

"Just a sec... wait, what?"

"He said something about the shore of the moon and that someone has him."

"Shit," she said. "Sorry. I mean, crap." She hung up the phone, walked over to Brandon and David, and sat with them on the floor. "What do we do?"

Maddie picked the phone up again, stared at it for a moment, then dialed Taysom. He did not answer, either.

***

Peter expects a stain, some sign, that Wally Raines had existed. The knife, safely closed, is all that remains. His hands are unbound, as are his feet. "Hello?" he says, expecting no answer, expecting all the answers.

Standing, the aches shudder through his body, nearly forcing him back onto the chair. There will be bruises, but he's alive. He's still here. Whatever took Wally spared him. Some people would block the memory out—the blackness, the screaming—but Peter hung onto it. All the years waiting to see a supernatural phenomenon, the time in Bern waiting for Diana to return...

He had no proof, of course. Not of the girl walking out of Moon Lake or of the black mass that swallowed a man before his eyes. His equipment was still on the shore.

On barely stable legs, Peter walks to the door and pushes it open. He still expects—*hopes*—to see some remnant of the blackness, but the forest is bright as it can be. Small shadows flit, animals or branches blown by the slight breeze. He surveys the immediate area, none of which looks familiar. Just how far did Wally drive from the lake to get here?

Drive!

Wally's truck must be close, but Peter can't see it from the stoop. Gently, he puts one foot then the next on the ground.

He walks, stumbles, leans over to take a deep breath. Finally at the back of the cabin, the last place the truck could be, Peter's heart sinks. The truck was there. What is left is something that once, recently, might have been a truck. What's left are four smoldering tires and a wad of metal crumpled up like a piece of paper ready to be thrown in the trash. From the top, Peter sees a pair of blue plastic testicles dangling as they did from the truck's tow hitch.

Peter tries to yell, to swear, but can't catch enough breath to get our more than a weak *fffuuu*. A blast of whiteness overcomes him, and as he returns to unconsciousness, he thinks *At least it's not the dark*. Leaves swirl around him, some sticking to his face, his clothes. The breeze whispers indecipherably, and squirrels hold conversations with birds a million miles away from Peter's awareness. *Thank God, it's not the dark.*

But darkness, the black mass, awaits him.

CHAPTER SIX

Traffic on Interstate 15 on a Saturday was not any better than it was on any other day. Once, when Taysom was a child, the speed limit had been 55, no one went anywhere on Sundays, and most Saturday traffic was from people going to or coming from Jazz basketball games in the spring, BYU or U of U football in the fall, or just visiting family during the summer. Salt Lake City boomed around him. The urban boom or houses, businesses, and people north of Salt Lake up to Ogden had already been there during those halcyon 55 miles per hour days. The southern boom was in full swing. Hotels, gas stations, weird tourist attractions, and houses everywhere clear into Blackhawk. He reached to secure the bulging file folder on the passenger seat. The air next to him chilled his fingertips. Briefly, he thought of images in the folder: drawings of Mormon pioneers crossing the plains, the grid layout for Blackhawk's city plan, photographs of Blackhawk's residents between 1890 and the Great Depression. Normal archive stuff.

The less than normal pages sat beneath these introductory files. Toombs needed them, but not for the reasons Toombs thought. They held a warning to someone like Toombs, a warning that Blackhawk will bury its secrets and anyone who digs them up. To Taysom, the warning was as bright as the brake lights right in front of him.

Taysom's feet reach for the brakes, but the space closed too quickly between the front of his car and rear of the car in front of him. At 70 miles per hour, the impact sent Taysom spinning. Had he spun into the barrier, he might have lived.

A Chevy Suburban—what he and his friends had called a Mormon Assault Vehicle—slammed into the passenger side, turning him back into the lane he'd previously occupied. Unfortunately, his space had been filled by a semi-truck. The wheels of the truck scraped Taysom's driver's side and soon the tires of the trailer had run him over, smashing down the roof of the car, pinning Taysom beneath it. Debris shredded the file folder on the passenger seat, the archives about Blackhawk meant for Toombs inside. The debris mixed with blood from Taysom and fluids from his car and the semi, covering the folder, beginning to seep into the pages. They were copies, but no one else knew what they meant.

No final words escaped Taysom's lips. His promises were broken. His life of faith and devotion now meant either everything or nothing. Those left behind would have to wait to know for sure.

As fire and ambulance crews worked to reach his body, Taysom's cellphone began to ring again. An EMT soon grasped the phone after fighting through the wreckage. The ringing had stopped, but the EMT hit redial.

"Grant, where are you? I can't reach Peter," Maddie's strained voice blared out.

"Ma'am, could you identify yourself please? Is this the owner of this phone's spouse?"

"What's going on? Who are you?"

"Ma'am, are you this man's spouse?"

"No, I'm just a friend."

"Ma'am, I'm going to need to let you go. You'll hear from someone soon."

"What's going on? Is Grant okay?

The EMT didn't hear Maddie's final question before hanging up. He handed the phone to a police officer. "This is never easy," he said, removing his blood-stained protective gloves and replacing them with a fresh pair.

***

"What's going on? Is Grant okay?" Maddie said into dead air. The connection had been broken, but she kept the phone to her ear. "Hello?"

"Blackhawk buries its secrets," David whispered nearby. "And anyone who digs them up."

Maddie dropped the phone, turned to her youngest son, and slapped him. The red from her hand appeared to float on the surface of his cheek rather the welling up from it.

"Mom, why did you do that?" Brandon asked. His own hands covered his cheeks, as if he'd been struck and not his little brother.

David said nothing, just sat and stared at Maddie. The rest of his face remained neutral, like he'd never opened his mouth. The mark of the slap dulled but didn't disappear. Not a single tear fell from David's eyes. His dry eyes burned instead, boring a whole first into Maddie, then Brandon.

"David? Sweetheart? Mommy's sorry," Maddie said. She held the hand that had struck her child in her other hand and felt it tingle. As Brandon sobbed in distress, she tilted her head, thinking to look closer at David's cheek. She caught his eyes again, smoldering with hatred on the surface, but to her eyes—the eyes of a mother—something else stirred beneath the disdain she saw.

"Get my hand mirror," she said. Brandon hiccupped a cry but didn't respond. "Brandon, go into the bathroom and get my hand mirror, please."

Nodding, Brandon obeyed and quickly returned, passing the small mirror to Maddie. She positioned herself behind David, hoping to see both their faces in the reflection. Her face, tear-streaked and puffy-eyed, floated near a head the size of David's. What she saw was not her son but was still familiar: the face of the devil from the painting she knew had been destroyed in a fire started by Brandon.

Maddie hoped to see her son. Staring back at her instead was the smiling face of Ruin.

***

With his camera set on level ground, Peter Toombs scans the area around him. He is in another neighborhood in Blackhawk, not far from a farm where two men who would eventually murder their sister-in-law and infant niece grew up. If he backtracks and heads west a few miles, he will see an out-of-place white building on the side of the mountain. It's a nightmare factory of its own and perhaps someday he will tell his version of that tale—how the lure of ancient Mormon treasure spurred two fanatics into a brutal murder—but today Peter is more interested in a lesser-known story out of Blackhawk's history. He faces the camera, clicks "record" on the remote in his pocket, and begins to speak.

"Battles and all-out wars were commonplace among the early Latter-day Saint settlers, not just in Blackhawk but all throughout the territory. Blackhawk itself vacillated between the names of two Native chiefs and briefly flirted with being named after an early citizen of the township. Hard feelings remained even after the dust settled and the

Mormons conquered the area. That sour relationship made it easy for some settlers to blame an Indigenous man for a series of horse thefts."

Peter pauses, knowing the network bosses may want him to edit some of this in post-production. He wants to get it right, but he also wants to get to the story.

"While a rash of accusations flew around, no solid evidence was provided to even arrest Johnny Two-Crows, as he was known by the citizens of the town. Cooler heads prevailed and Two-Crows was never seen by another white person in the Utah Territory. But the horse thefts—a crime fit for capital punishment due to its ability to disrupt the livelihood of the owners—continued."

Another brief pause, and Peter lets the suspense build. He's telling himself this story and he wants to hit just right.

"In 1890, six years before Utah became a state, Cassandra Wright and her son Beckett, lived together on a farm where I'm standing now, on the edge of modern Blackhawk and then far enough from town for the Wrights not to be bothered most days. Heathcliff Wright had abandoned his wife and only child years before, leaving them to tend to the land he'd staked out upon their arrival in the valley. One day, desperate for answers, small groups of men from town were sent to the outlying farms and homesteads. Such a group came upon the Beckett farmstead, but before they reached the front door, a party member recognized his own horse, stolen from its stable six months prior. While he wanted to rush the home, the other men convinced him to do things lawfully. While two men went to see if any other stolen horses were on the property, three others, including the wronged man, approached the house and knocked on the door. They could her voices and what sounded to them like violence. 'God

Almighty,' the record indicates the party leader said, Beckett Wright is beating his mother to death.'"

One last pause and Peter knows this is when he must truly sell this story. Will it shock viewers who've become jaded by so many other true crime documentaries and podcasts? Will the network choose to dramatize this moment? As long as they don't cut it, Peter thinks.

"The men burst through the door, following the sounds of what they believe is a murder in the moment. What they find, instead, is mother and son together in the throes of love-making. Yes, they heard flesh violently beating against flesh, but this was not what they expected. Outside, the evidence of horse thievery against Cassandra and Beckett mounted. Inside, Beckett mounted Cassandra."

Peter hits the "stop" button on the remote and laughs at his own bad joke. "Screw it," he says aloud, "I'm leaving it." He shakes himself and regains his narrator poise.

"Stealing horses, a horrible crime, could still be understood if not condoned. Engaging in such an act of intimacy with one's own mother and vice versa, one's own son, was unforgivable and intolerable to these men of God. Pistols were drawn on the obviously defenseless Wrights and they were soon bound to the bed they had shared. The three men exited the house, gathered their two compatriots and came to a decision.

"As soon as all the horses were gathered, the ones that were known to be stolen property and even animals that may have legally belonged to the Wrights, the men set fire to the house. Cassandra and Beckett Wright died in the blaze. Their farmstead was far enough from the rest of the township that no fire brigade, such as it was, was called for nor sent. The fire burned quickly, leaving nothing but piles of smoldering rubble. Somewhere in that rubble were the bodies of Cassandra and Beckett Wright, burned to death for stealing horses and incest."

Peter hits "stop" again and collects himself. Good Mormon folk, he thinks. He doesn't condone the crimes the Wrights allegedly committed but on the spot vigilante justice is never the answer, either. He thumbs "record" for a closing thought.

"While the names of Cassandra Wright and her son Beckett are included in the official town records—including the charge of horse theft and incest—the initial cause of death was noted as accidental in the course of a citizens' arrest. The names of the men involved were removed from all documents concerning the matter."

The recording ends, and Peter looks around him. He knows the families who divvied up the Wrights' homestead and can guess who their descendants are, some spread throughout the state and many still right here in Blackhawk. Smalltown secrets are a dime a dozen, he knows, but he also knows there are hungry viewers with pockets full of coins.

He also knows there is a good chance that one of his own ancestors could have lit the fire that murdered the Wrights more than a century ago.

There is only more stop on his list of haunts. He's not going to the famous places, like seeing the ghostly gravedigger in Salt Lake City, or the haunted hotel in Ogden. His final story is about a little girl who drowned in a lake in the mountains.

There is one stop along the way, however.

CHAPTER SEVEN

"Are you really going up there," Maddie asked from her porch, watching Peter load his car with the equipment he had taken out to show the boys.

"Debbie asked me the same thing," Peter said, checking a strap and not making eye contact with Maddie. "I have to. People keep asking me to explain what happened and I can't. I don't know what happened. Those people in Bern should have been just like us; just people in small town Utah, living life, going to church, swearing occasionally, and giving directions to lost skiers. But something was wrong there. I was too caught up in my own shit—" He peered toward Brandon and David, huddled over Pokémon cards, to see if they heard him swear and saw no reaction. "Sorry. Habit. Anyway, I was in my own head so much that I didn't see what was coming. I tried to make sense of it the best I could, but there's still something missing."

"You still miss her."

Peter let the statement hang in the air between them. He knew it wasn't a question. There wasn't a question to ask. He still missed Diana Ward and always would.

"I used to read those trashy romances," Maddie continued, breaking the awkward moment. "My ex hated them, but they were fun. If you wrote those, we'd kiss right now, but..."

"But this isn't that kind of story. I know that, too." Peter closed the trunk, walked over to Maddie, and put his hand on her shoulder. "I don't have another love story in me, but it would be something to get to know you." His hand lingered on her shoulder and she smiled. "Maybe next time."

"Next time?"

"Yeah. The sequel, right? Mysterious man shows up at the end, sets up the next installment. Happens all the time in Hollywood. Sometimes we even get the budget to make the follow-up."

Maddie laughed hard. She didn't know anything about Hollywood budgets and imagined Peter was making up most of what he knew. But it felt right. The whole moment felt right.

"Mr. Toombs," Brandon said, shaking the adults out of their brief revery. "Do you think Charizard could beat a T-Rex?"

"I don't know, but I'd pay to see it," Peter said.

"I think the T-Rex would win," Maddie said. "David, what do you—"

David had fallen down, silently, as the others talked. He lay stiff on the lawn, blades of grass brushing his cheeks. A ladybug crawled on one hand. His eyes were open but only showed the whites.

"David!" Maddie jumped to her son, her feet barely touching the ground between them. She knelt and remembered her gift: she could pray for Heavenly Father to intercede and with the Priesthood inside her, make miracles. "David. Listen, honey. Can you hear me?"

As she spoke, Peter and Brandon moved nearby. Maddie grabbed Brandon's hand. "Put your hands on your brother's head, son. You're going to help me."

The teen boy did as his mother commanded. Placing his hands on his brother's head, Brandon could feel heat coming through David's hair. As he pressed harder, the heat became icy. He tried to focus on his mother's words—familiar words he'd heard a hundred times, but so unfamiliar coming from his own mom's mouth—but the new coldness of David's crown pulled his attention away. His mind drifted and he recalled running the summer before. Running past the downtown stores and into the cemetery, into the open tomb—

"Brandon! Come back," Maddie whisper-shouted. "We need you."

"Yes, Mom. I'm here. I'm here."

"Keep your hands on his head no matter what happens," she ordered. As she finished, David's legs began to kick out, pulling up and thrusting back, a piston stuck in place.

"Should I hold his legs," Peter asked.

"No, just... just stay out of the way," Maddie said with more kindness than she felt.

Tugging at his gloves, Peter backed away. He wanted to grab his camera, record this for the show—an LDS blessing in action, he knew; a step in an exorcism, he hoped and hoped against. Whatever that fleeting feeling just before was, Peter knew taking his camera out now would be the end to it. Instead, he grabbed a water bottle not yet packed in the car and set it near enough to Maddie that she'd know it was there without him having to say anything.

The words of the blessing continued to be soft but demanding. Peter could hardly make them out. They felt comforting and familiar, as they had to Brandon, but also out of place. A woman invoking Priesthood authority didn't happen in this culture. He'd read Maddie's disciplinary documents, the ones she shared that is, and knew she could get into trouble with the church for this. Trouble didn't matter. David did.

"Keep your hands in place, Brandon," Maddie shouted. Her oldest son did not waver, she saw, but needed to remind him just to say something different from the prayer. At this point, however, every word out of her mouth and in her heart was part of her prayer.

David's thrusting subsided to a twitch and his upper body never moved. Peter leaned in, taking a small kick to the shin for his curiosity.

"This we pray in the name of Jesus Christ, Amen," Maddie said.

"Amen," Brandon echoed.

Reflexively, Peter added his own agreement. "Amen."

They stayed still and silent for what seemed like hours. After about ninety seconds, David spoke. "Amen," he said. He turned to his side and began to snore.

"Help me get him inside," Maddie said. Peter knew she was talking to him. He hoisted the boy—David's body cold in some spots and warm in others—and followed Maddie into the house and David's bedroom.

Still outside, Brandon remained kneeling. He'd folded his arms and began his own prayer. "Dear Heavenly Father. Please let David be well. Whatever had us last summer, if that's what is in him, push it out. Please, Lord. Help my brother. In Jesus' name, Amen."

***

Taysom's body, wrecked as much as his car, arrived at the hospital without the flurry of action one might see when EMTs and doctors are trying to save someone. He wasn't wheeled into emergency surgery or straight into the ICU. He went right to the morgue.

The few items in his car were packaged into a file box, ready for someone to retrieve at their convenience. The files Taysom had collected were meant to guide Peter Toombs and keep him from looking in places that might only bring him harm. Flipping through the pages, the morgue attendant saw words he couldn't piece together. Some he knew but they didn't make sense. Blood atonement. Harper, England. Something about a pioneer wagon train. There was one paper that looked like a copy of a newspaper, a story about Bern, the fake Swiss village near Heber City. He'd gone with his parents there one winter before the Olympics made it impossible to enjoy. He'd had a hot cocoa and bought a guidebook at the bookstore. The news article didn't look like it was good news, though. Covered in blood and shredded by broken glass, nothing ever does.

***

Peter waited until Maddie had David tucked in and Brandon comfortably posted in front of the TV. A brightly-colored animated show flickered there, but Brandon didn't seem to be paying that much attention. Peter's concern for the family felt odd considering how short the time had been since he met them. He'd intruded on their recovery from tragedy—the deaths of people they were close to, a fire, the investigations that followed from law enforcement and the church—only to bring those things right back into their lives. That moment before David's seizure between Maddie and Peter was just that, a moment.

"Like dust in the wind," Peter muttered.

"You aren't in Kansas anymore," Maddie said, somehow snagging Peter's near-silent comment out of the air.

"Kansas, that great metaphor for home, is a place I haven't been for a long time," Peter said.

"I've never been to Kansas. I've barely ever left Utah," Maddie said.

"I mean, I haven't felt like I was home in years. Even Blackhawk doesn't feel like home anymore."

"And that's why you have to go? Why you're making a show about all the town's dirty little secrets? So that it never feels like home again?"

He was stunned. "When you say it like that, yes. There's something wrong here and has been for a long time. I don't know what it is but it makes it so I can't live here. I can't live in Bern, either. I don't know that L.A. will have me back if this project tanks."

"Lost in the desert because something on the other side of the river scared you."

"A poor wayfaring stranger."

"Joseph Smith preferred 'A Poor Wayfaring Man of Grief.' I think that's you. Chasing ghosts until you become one."

"You fill me with confidence." Peter smiled, hoping a bit of sarcasm would ease the tension he felt building up. Maddie, ever the schoolteacher, didn't bite.

"I mean it," Maddie said. "You'll chase a ghost or a de—a dev—shit. I can't even say it."

"Chase a demon or the devil…" Peter filled in.

"Yes. You'll follow them right into your own grave, thinking that will make you happy. Other people have to live and find a way to make things better even when they know the evil in the world. Some of us are closer to it than we wish. You wouldn't even be here if you weren't on your demon hunt."

Peter turned away as Maddie covered her face and began to cry into her hands. As much as he wanted to reach out and comfort her, he couldn't. He couldn't get into her life any deeper than he already was. Her story was there, but he wasn't ready to tell it.

"I'm sorry, Maddie. I don't know how to make you not hurt, or how to help your kids. You are a healer; I'm just a carnival barker showing people the geek show."

Between hitches of crying, Maddie snorted a laugh. "You used that line in your book. Except you were the geek. Now you are just the host and not the attraction. Does that make us the entertainment?"

"That's not what I meant."

"You should go. You have somewhere else to be."

"I'll call you and check in."

"Yes, please do that. The boys will want to hear from you."

Maddie didn't watch Peter drive away. After he left, she went to the spot where David had fallen earlier. Peter's water bottle was there, but something was wrong. The plastic bottle was misshapen, as if it had been run through the dishwasher and melted.

***

He doesn't feel the first tendrils of the blob tug at the cuff of his pants. Like a tentacle, the black mass wraps around Peter's ankle before flattening and covering his calf like a cast. The fabric of his pants bursts from the pressure and still he feels nothing. He's floating, he would think if he had thoughts at this moment. There is nothing but emptiness and for the first time, Peter can't even feel his heartbeat. He expects the giant of his childhood to return, the pulsing and plodding of the great monster's footsteps to waken him out of this nightmare, but there is nothing. There is neither discomfort nor soothing.

Until the blackness tightens, that is. The covering on his right leg squeezes and Peter is jolted back into his body as if he had been hit with a defibrillator. The shock is not so much electric as it is cold. In his returning consciousness, Peter expects to be warm. *Surely I must have pissed myself*, he thinks, noting his own interior haughty tone. *Indeed, this is all bullshit.*

The mass is not bullshit and it squeezes again, forcing Peter to sit up. He doesn't know where he is; he is blind. Then he knows he needs to open his eyes. This thought, one he can't recall having before, comes from outside himself. It's coming from the blob, the black mass that brought him back from emptiness. He's never had to tell himself to open his eyes or remind himself to draw a single breath. He had, during the worst of his grief after Diana died, reminded himself to live, to get up, and to not become a broken and bitter man. He had to tell himself that the bonfires and the deaths in Bern— even Judge Lerner's smashed in face—weren't his fault. Wally Reins might disagree, but the death of Wally's uncle wasn't Peter's fault. No one told the Blackhawk detective to check on Peter in Bern. He just showed up. And Wally, well, Wally shouldn't have kidnapped Peter and tortured him.

Wally! Thinking of the disintegrated Wally, plucked from existence by the black mass that now surrounded Peter, feels like Peter's first original thought ever. That one comes from inside him and it comes out with a scream.

The scream pours from Peter's deepest places, mentally and physically. The mass stops squeezing as if surprised by the outburst. Peter screams until his dry throat clenches and his stomach churns. He will not vomit, he's harder than that—

another purely Peter thought. His stomach disagrees. He is turned to the side by the black blob which surrounds him, not as tightly but still firmly. Bile and spit foam out of Peter's mouth but not much else. He retches, his body heaving with pain and shock. A tendril of the mass crawls up Peter's back and an airy portion covers his lips, gently wiping away the spew from his mouth. The gesture is almost loving and Peter pulls back from it but has nowhere to go.

He still doesn't know exactly where he is. He was in a cabin. He was in the back of Wally's truck before that, he thinks. On the shore recording first, seeing the little drowned girl. Did he see her? Did he get her on camera?

Does it matter?

A sharp pain courses through his midsection but is soon covered by the mass. The blob has filled a knife wound that reopened during Peter's retching. A brief vision of bleeding out in the middle of the woods comes to Peter and he is sure he will die. He leaves no one to remember him. His work... nothing to write home about, he thinks with a bitter irony. The mass clamps down upon and he first thinks it is feeding on his despair. Another cinch and a new thought runs from his toes to his brain like an old telegraph message: you aren't here to die.

Not yet, anyway.

The *not yet* slams Peter in his most motivating area: anger. He screams again with rage instead of pain. Rage at Wally for doing this to him, rage at the mass for not communicating well, and rage at Maddie Smith and her sons for...

For giving him a reason to come back to Utah and Blackhawk just to be confronted with the garbage he thought he'd left behind in Bern.

***

Yes, he was going there. The canyon road to Moon Lake passed Bern. One could take a left almost midway between Blackhawk and Moon Lake and be in Bern ten minutes later. Or one could wave at the sign pointing toward the village and its hospitality and drive right by.

Or one could stop before turning, keeping the signal on even though this was Utah, because no other cars were on the road and gaze down the road to Bern and wonder just why in the hell anyone would want to go back there after what happened to him. Him, Peter thought, him being me. Why would I want to go back there? He grasped the door handle in his left hand and his keys in his right, ready to turn the car off and walk around a bit, maybe kick the sign for good luck, and then decide. He could hear the rumble of an old pick-up truck coming up behind him, some redneck on the way to his fishing hole. Peter let go of both objects he held and put his hands on the steering wheel.

"Ten and two," he said, before letting his two o'clock hand tap the radio button. No more grunge, like the first time he'd taken this turn. An audiobook began somewhere in the middle of a chapter. An ancient voice spoke of a young priest and an old one, fighting to purge a demon from a girl somewhere between the ages of Brandon and David Smith. Peter loved the book, it comforted him. Books read by their authors were his favorite. The voice filled Peter's car and he knew this trip to Bern and Moon Lake would make or break him in Hollywood. If he failed, he had that new manuscript to fall back on, the one about his short time in Bern.

Finally making the left turn, Peter gunned his engine loud enough that he neither heard nor saw Wally Reins slow and pull over near the sign marking the way to Bern.

Peter knew right away something had changed. The blues were faded and missing in places peeled away from the trims of houses and shops. Windows were boarded over and trash skirted across the street in front of him as he drove. He cruised past the diner, no Wilkommen greetings today. The shingle for The Bern Bookseller, Ben Hill Prop. swung on one hook, dangling precariously over the sidewalk. One more stiff wind would send crashing through the window, shattering it like gunfire.

But there wasn't a window, Peter knew. Gunfire a decade before had indeed shattered it, killing the eponymous Ben Hill with shots meant for Peter. His shins and forearms crackled with the memory of crawling over broken glass, better to suffer a few scrapes on his arms and legs than expose himself to the sniper aiming for his head. He'd made it out, made it to the house on the hill that had held a sense of twisted hope at the time; he'd survived.

Bern, by all accounts, did not. When the bodies of two prominent citizens were linked to a murdered police officer, among others, the rest of the residents must have scattered. Like Maddie after the fire and the deaths of Blaine Griffen and Rey Montoya, Peter Toombs spent his fair share of time being interviewed, questioned, grilled, and suspected. He'd paid a fine although he couldn't recall what it was for and lived with the scars and pains from broken arms since then. If he wanted to remember, he only had to look at his black-gloved hands. If his life had become like a *giallo*, one of those 1970s Italian slasher films, he definitely would have been the killer.

He was just a regular guy going through some stuff, he told himself then and now. Grief will make a person buy a house in their dead girlfriend's hometown if they can afford it. Not just any house, either. HER house. Doing so brought him nothing but more heartache. He never saw Diana again.

Ghosts aren't real, he knew, except those we carry in our hearts. Those ghosts will kill you if you let them.

School zone-slow, Peter drove along Main Street looking for any sign of life. The house he'd bought lived in and sold again bore down on him from the hill on his right. To his left loomed the Bern Cemetery gates. The chain that had once attempted to block his entry lay on the ground, covered in dirt and tumbleweeds. The weeds crunched beneath his tires. No signage about the state of the cemetery appeared, and the rage that ran most of Peter's life resurfaced. How could they leave this place untended? Had they no respect for the dead?

Rage dissipated as Peter remember exactly what Lerner and the other residents of Bern thought of their deceased loved ones. They were but pawns in a game Peter never learned all the rules to. Even Debbie Ward, kidnapped and used as a surrogate for her sister Diana, was never sure what they had the night they first buried her alive and "resurrected" her. It just wasn't something either of them ever talked about.

As he traveled farther into the cemetery—cemeteries stand alone, graveyards are connected to churches passed along his train of thought—he noticed patches of mown grass. Not every headstone had been cleared, creating little islands of care around some markers and leaving others to the ravages of time. The boulder marking Diana's grave was one such island. A ten-foot circle had been mown down around her marker but Peter could see that the weather had taken a toll on the granite. The stone wasn't as tall as he remembered and the once rough-hewn top and back had been worn smooth by wind. He made a mental note to ask Debbie who'd come here to maintain the site and then it hit him: it didn't matter who was doing it because he was paying for it. He'd started that account and was pleased to see the duty he'd financed continued despite the abandonment of the town. Briefly, he worried about the sprinklers turning on, but soon conceded that wouldn't be an issue. As he sat at the foot of the grave, he noticed the dryness of the grass. One wrong spark would set the whole place on fire. Bern would burn.

That wasn't as funny as a part of him wanted it to be. Sick jokes at the expense of others were best left to teenagers who hadn't had their own asses kicked by life yet. Soon enough, we all are broken.

As he ruminated, trying to delve into happy memories instead of the nightmares of his brief time in Bern, a wayward pebble struck Peter's hand. He brushed it away but soon another rolled its way against his pinkie. A dozen or so pebbles followed, and Peter saw they were pieces of Diana's headstone, flaking off and rolling down the hill. He watched the run of loose granite spill beyond the mown area surround the marker and disappear into the overgrown grass and weeds. Curious, he stood and followed the barely discernable trail the pebbles made the edge of the small clearing. Just past the dividing line of maintained lawn and untouched meadow, a pile of pebbles had formed. At first, Peter thought the pile was random, just a bunch of rocks building up where they could. He was almost right.

The pebbles, as he now saw, had lined the rim of an open grave. The grass had grown in the hole, too, and more pebbles and other detritus had collected at the bottom. Peter glanced back over his shoulder toward Diana's marker, her chiseled profile as poignant as the first time he saw it, when the wind he worried about came tumbling down from the mountains and across the meadow. Staring uphill, Peter lost his balance and fell into the grave he knew to be the hole the citizens of Bern had dug Debbie out of. His back landed on rotting wood from the bonfire and what was left of it disintegrated on contact. A mouse jumped from the commotion and ran up Peter's leg before bounding out of the hole. That was a good sign; a mouse meant a rattlesnake had not chosen the grave as its burrow. Something crawled beneath Peter and he hoped it was only earthworms. He shot his hands up to grip the walls of dirt, holding back any panic. When another hand gripped one of his, panic flooded in.

***

Smoke from the wildfires wafted over Blackhawk and some families in the neighborhood began to pack for an evacuation. David sat on the floor, smiling from some angles and frowning from others, sometimes whistling but mostly remaining silent. The mirror dropped from Maddie's hand and she was sure it would break, but the shatterproof handle hit the floor first. She yelped in anticipation of the crashing that didn't come.

"Brandon, keep trying to reach Peter, okay, honey?" She tried to remain calm, for Brandon's sake and for David's, if he could hear her. She reached to hold his face in her hands, but the heat from his cheeks burned like the fires nearby and she couldn't touch him. "Plug in the phone, too. Just in case."

Just in case had come. *Worst case scenario* was now. Griffen and Montoya couldn't help her. Taysom, who'd become a rock and foundation, was dead. Peter Toombs, the newest man in her life, bailed out for some stupid adventure into a stupid town that didn't deserve his attention. She may not have earned the writer's attention or affection, but she needed him now.

"It keeps going to voicemail," Brandon said.

"Keep trying. Keep trying until he answers." Brandon mumbled a reply but Maddie didn't catch it. She knew he was scared, but she also knew he had good reason to be. Ruin, as the entity had called itself, had been inside Brandon, too. It had changed both their lives, brought them closer—no reason to be thankful for how—and they were the ones who had to face it again.

David, hot to the touch, reddened. He didn't move but his skin first became flushed then a deep red as if he'd been in the sun for hours. Not just his face, but his hands and any other exposed skin peeking out of his clothes. Maddie pushed away from him as he began to boil from the inside.

"Get some water," she shouted, rushing into the kitchen and bumping into Brandon. "Get the bucket from the closet and fill it up." Maddie opened the refrigerator and hoisted a gallon of water out, spinning the lid off as she rushed back to David's side. She could hear Brandon following her directions as she poured the water over David's head, not caring about his clothes or the carpet. At first, the water steamed away before touching David. As the jug emptied, a few drops escaped the heat of the air but sizzled and left small burn marks on David, pinpoints of white on his otherwise red flesh. Brandon arrived with the five-gallon bucket, water splashing over the edges. Maddie tossed the empty gallon aside, steadied the bucket carried by Brandon and counted three before dumping it all onto David.

The liquid overwhelmed the boy. He tipped over just as the bucket had tipped out its contents over him. He writhed and hissed as his clothes and skin steamed, but the redness abated and the water left a few wet spots on his clothes. His hair, which took the brunt of both the single gallon and the bucket, remained dry. Kicking, screaming, his mouth chomping at nothing but air, David lost the last bit of control he had. His bowels and bladder emptied, joining the growing stench of soggy clothes and steaming water. Outside, ash began to fall on houses in the nearby blocks. Sirens roared to life and the noise of neighbors leaving their homes behind grew to a steady pulse. Doors slammed, engines revved, tires peeled; the Smiths were left alone to face a demon once again.

CHAPTER EIGHT

David slept the rest of the day after Peter left for Bern and Moon Lake. He felt like sleeping all the time, but he also never wanted to sleep. When he was asleep, he saw horrible things. He didn't think they were dreams. He saw a great fire rushing down the canyon and consuming all of Blackhawk. He saw wild animals burning and dying. He saw people running from the flames and burning alive just as the deer and rabbits did. He saw the house that had scared Brandon so much as it was before Brandon burned it down. People in Pioneer clothes like he had seen at the Blackhawk Museum build the house in his mind, a man with a large belly and a wide grin directed others in the construction. David didn't like that man, especially when he turned and smiled at David. The boy couldn't hear the words, but he was sure the man was inviting David into the home even before it was completed.

Then he saw the man kneeling in an open barn, horses and hay nearby, his hands bound behind his back. Another man circled the first, carrying a long, shiny knife. He mouthed two words that David couldn't make out. For some reason, David felt sorry for the man with the knife, even though he knew the knife would be used on the larger man. Above this scene, he saw Ruin, his mouth chanting more words David couldn't hear. Was the gnarled, red and black beast chanting to the bound man or the man with the knife? David didn't know and didn't want to know. His own hands felt tied, lashed to his body keeping him from moving, from breaking away from this vision. As he struggled, Ruin seemed to notice him, looked at him from inside his own head, and smiled. His long, black tongue snaked out between burnt lips and the tip flicked into one crusty nostril. Ruin swallowed whatever it was he'd found there then spoke to David. Still not hearing anything, David shrugged, the first real motion he could remember making in hours. Ruin sailed down from his ceiling perch, not touching the standing man nor the kneeling, and settled in front of David's consciousness. He spoke again and the words appeared as if in a comic book. The word bubbles were black and the letters red: *Do not forsake them, David. They know not what they do.*

At last, a sound as the final letter appeared, but David would have traded all sounds not to hear these again. Ruin's laughter joined the noise of the bound man's entrails spilling onto the ground and the other man walking away, his work complete. David couldn't see the bound man's body, but he could see that one hand had been loosened and the knife the other man had held slipping from his fingers. *It's a nightmare, David,* came another word bubble, even as the cacophony of Ruin's laughter continued. *It's all in your head, just like I am.*

Just before Ruin could reach out and ensnare David's mind fully, a black cloud seeped through the gaps in the dream-barn's roof. The cloud first covered the now dead man in the middle of the floor, then found its way to Ruin's feet. It pulled at the demon's limbs, slowly swallowing him. David could feel his mind and body being released simultaneously, but he knew he wasn't totally free. This was a reprieve, a word that floated into David's mind from the dark cloud that surrounded Ruin.

Finally, he slept for real and did not dream.

***

The hand pulled Peter out the grave with unyielding strength. The ease with which Peter went from the bottom of a pit to the flat ground unsettled him more than finding the open grave did.

"Do you know me," the man said before Peter had a chance to even look at him. "I look awfully familiar, don't I?"

"You took the words right out of my mouth, friend," Peter said. "Do I know you?" He brushed grave dirt off his clothes and titled his head to see a stocky man, well over six feet tall, grinning down at him. There was an air of familiarity about the man, but Peter could not place him. Instead, he stood up, reached out his hand again, and waited for a shake.

"You're that writer guy, right? Used to live up on the hill?" The grin receded, but the voice remained pleasant. Not childlike, but genuinely happy to see another living human.

"I am. Peter. You are?"

"Wrong. You don't know me. I saw you around that summer but couldn't stand to say hello. I wasn't as big then, and my mom scared me off of talking to you. I see your fellow out here cutting the grass and I never doubted you'd come back and see if he was doing the job. He does, I am happy to report. Couldn't hurt him every now and again to spruce up the rest of the lot, but I don't suppose you pay him for that."

Peter dropped his hand, getting neither the handshake nor a name from the man before him. "I'd almost forgotten that I did pay for the upkeep, truth be told. I didn't expect the town to be so desolate. You mentioned your mom. Is she still here?"

"Oh, she's around here someplace." The grin returned for a split second but Peter read pain in it. "Just over yonder." The man nodded toward another grave island, the grass shaven down around a smaller headstone.

"Is anyone else still in town," Peter asked.

"Nah. Heck, I'm not even here all the time. I just come by to scare off the lookie-loos and to wait for you. I got a two-fer today. Some weirdo in a pick-up came up after you, slowed down a bit too much but gunned it out when I showed him this..." The man reached behind his back and pulled out a horror-movie worthy machete. "I have to use it in some spots to clear the tumbles, but it always does the trick when the punks from down the mountain rear up."

The blade did its job on Peter, too. *I've stepped out of my own book into one of those backwoods slasher movies*, he thought. *If I'm going to die, this is as good a place as any.*

"I keep it clean, of course. Sharpen it good when I get home." The man raised the long machete and cut the air in front of Peter. "It's plenty strong but I don't think it'd lop off anybody's head like in those shows you like."

"Thank God for that."

"Yeah, that's true. But don't say things like that. Good boy Albert says good things and hears good things. We never take the Lord's name in vain."

"Albert? That's your name?"

"Albert Moser, Mr. Toombs. It's been fun finally meeting you, but I have to tend to Mother now. Don't you go falling into any more holes." With that, Albert Moser hid his machete in a sheath on his back and trundled away from Peter. "I'd watch out for that pick-up, though. Squirrely-looking punk driving it. I might have seen him up here before, but I can't recall correctly."

Squirrely-looking punks in pick-up trucks are the least of my worries. Machete-toting brutes, it seems, are off the list of concerns, too, Peter thought. Something about the name the hulk gave rang familiar, like Peter should have known him. He had other ghosts to chase, however.

Kicking up dirt clods and crunching over tumbleweeds, Peter returned to his car. The paint was dustier than he liked seeing it, but that meant he was out living. If you have time for a carwash, you have too much time. Leaving Bern— again, finally—he didn't think he had time for such frivolity. Washing the car could wait. Moon Lake lay ahead and maybe he'd finally see his ghost.

The audiobook started up as he pulled out of the decrepit fake Swiss village. The mother was screaming at the priests to do anything they could. That reminded him of Maddie and he hoped he didn't give her the wrong impression when he left. Yes, he liked her, but he knew he wouldn't be any good for her. He wanted to write her story, something along the lines of the book he listened to now, if she'd let him. But first, one last stop to check off the list.

Albert Moser watched Peter Toombs leave Bern. He did remember the man from all those years ago and how much trouble he'd left in his wake. He'd wanted nothing more than to plow through Peter's neck with his machete, but he couldn't. He'd made a deal with the man in the pick-up truck. The punk said he'd take care of Peter and promised to bring Albert a souvenir: one of Peter's hands. That was good enough. He'd wait, not too long he hoped. For now, he cleared away the small clumps of dirt and gravel that had fallen his mother's grave and laid down on the coffin. He reached into a hole in the side and touched her rotting body. This would always be home.

A snake weaved along his mother's body and around his fingers, using Albert's arm like a tree limb to climb out of the coffin. The snake coiled around Albert's forearm, constricted for just a moment, then continued on its way. Albert smiled. He was happy his mother was someone else's home now, too.

***

Brandon gripped the bucket, waiting for Maddie's instructions. Watching his brother fog up like the barrels of homemade root beer they used to make didn't make him feel any better about the situation. The burning he knew about; he'd had that creep inside him, but the thought they'd gotten rid of it. Somehow, a piece had gotten into David, and Brandon felt like it was his fault. "Mom, what.."

"Shh... shh another bit, baby," Maddie said. She hesitated to let Brandon out of the room, even just to refill the water bucket. If David started convulsing again, she wanted Brandon right there to hold him down and she would... what would she do? "Don't take your eyes off of him."

"Mom?" Brandon didn't always question Maddie but she was getting used to it.

"Just watch him." Maddie went into the kitchen, opened one cupboard then another. From these, she removed a small glass tumbler and a bottle of olive oil. She poured a measure of oil into the tumbler and held that in her hands. "Let's hope this helps."

Her eyes closed and the prayer began as naturally as a common blessing over a meal. "Oh, God, by the power of the Melchizedek Priesthood which I hold, I consecrate this oil for the use of healing of the sick and for..." She couldn't believe she was saying it, but there was no stopping now. "And for the casting out of demons. I ask that thy Holy Spirit work through me and this oil to rid thy son David of any earthly sickness which has befallen him and to drive the demon plaguing him back into the arms of Lucifer, where they can burn together. In the name of Heavenly Father, the Son Jesus Christ, and the Holy Ghost. Amen."

As she opened her eyes, the golden liquid appeared to clear, as if any impurities were being sifted out by an unseen sieve. A scent like candles—different from the wildfire smell from outside—floated before her. A sense of calmness came over her as if a thick quilt had been draped over her shoulders. She'd not felt peace like this since—

"Mom!"

At once, the silence collapsed around her, but the peace remained. That quilt was the Holy Ghost riding with her into battle.

"Mom! It's David, he's—"

David hung suspended in the air, waist high to Brandon and Maddie both. His body had not changed positions, rather he had ascended into the empty space without hurry or impediment. Brandon dropped the bucket and for a second, it looked like it would roll under David. As it neared the spot David had occupied moments before, the bucket came to a complete stop, then rolled the opposite direction, out of the way.

"What do we do, Mom," Brandon said, the pleasing in his voice matched by that on his face.

"We pray, son. We pray until this ends." Maddie took position at David's head and poured the consecrated oil onto his head, careful not to drip it on the floor. David's dry hair glistened with the oil. After placing the tumbler on the floor, Maddie laid hands on David's head, covering most of the area the oil had spread. "Put your hands on mine. If a prayer comes to you, say it. Get ready to have other thoughts try to take hold of you. They'll be the worst things you can imagine, but remember this: they are the devil's thoughts, not yours."

Brandon did as asked, moving next to his mother, putting his hands on top of Maddie's. Together they pleaded with Heavenly Father to heal David, to release him from this torment. They commanded Ruin, the devil's demon, to be gone from David, from their house, from Blackhawk, and from the entire earthly realm. As the wildfire licked the homes mere blocks away, the Smith family remained locked in a spiritual battle.

As the fire began eating away at Blackhawk and the Smiths waged their war, Peter Toombs grappled with his own brand of demons.

CHAPTER NINE

The sky above him should be clearing, he thinks. It's daytime, isn't it? As the enveloping darkness subsides, Peter's body responds as if he's woken up on a summer day, ready to find new adventures and maybe get into a little bit of trouble. He feels like it should be dawn. He can't tell what time it is. The sun is blocked by clouds but they do not prevent a certain light of day from reaching Peter's eyes. The world is diffuse, it's gray, it smells like he burnt dinner again.

"I'm so sorry, Diana," he speaks. "We'll have to get takeout."

Speaking aloud jolts Peter from the fugue state he's been in since Wally Reins sliced his knife across his arm. The black mass, the blob of pain and healing is gone. He stands upright, his joints releasing days of pent-up tension. He can see the rips and cuts in his clothes but beneath them is only his normal pale white skin. No blood, no scabs, no scars. He has been picked clean by a wound scavenger, one that could kill if it so desired.

"What are you," he says, but doesn't expect answer. He is alone under a smoky sky, lost but unafraid. The mass took his fear, for now. Forever? No, not likely. What good is a horror writer who isn't scared of something?

Walk.

He hears the word and knows it is coming from some vestige the black mass left behind inside him. He turns a full circle, unsure which way to walk. As he regains his initial position, he hears it again, as if his feet are speaking to him.

Walk.

He walks and as he does, he feels the heat of the sky and the push of the wildfires devouring the land around him. He hears an airplane, one of those large planes ready to dump fire retardant on the forest. Is that stuff toxic? If he's under the drop zone, will it make him sick?

If I was under the drop zone, I'd be dead. Burnt to a crisp. I must not be too far away from the fire line, though.

He's right about that, he knows—from himself and from the soundless guide inside him. The gray sky isn't clouds, it's smoke, and if he doesn't hurry he'll die from breathing the smoke before a flame ever touches him. He hears sirens and chatter but he can't see the location of the clamor.

Run. Now.

Not hesitating, Peter picks up speed. He doesn't think running with lungs full of contaminated air is healthy but the other options are worse. He runs. He doesn't look back even when he hears the bursting of pinecones and acorns, like popcorn, in the heat. He runs past trees that scrape his forearms and cheeks. He runs, miraculously not tripping over fallen branches or stepping in rabbit burrows. He runs until he thinks he can't run anymore and runs beyond that.

Peter Toombs, always running from something, runs for his life.

He sprints, a final push before he knows his body will give out on him, pumping his arms and legs further than he ever knew possible. He chugs and chugs, ready to quit, knowing he can't quit. The giant, now carrying an aspen tree torch, is hot on his tail. He runs until he sees lights flash before his eyes, the stars that indicate he's run out of breath and will now succumb to the darkness once again.

But lights ae not what he thinks he will see when he sinks into unconsciousness. The lights are red and blue, red and blue. The lights have sounds, a blaring siren and loud voices talking over each other, to each other, to other disembodied voices in other places. Peter runs and doesn't stop until he sees a miracle right in front of him. A red firetruck, the source of the brightest lights and loudest noises, is the miracle. On the door, Peter sees

BLACKHAWK FD No. 1

He wants to laugh. How did he get so far? How far did Wally drive him away from the shore of Moon Lake?

How did he find his way home?

"Sir? Sir, are you injured?" One of those voices talks to Peter but he needs just a moment to register he is being spoken to. "Sir, do you need assistance?"

Peter gives the firefighter Maddie's address; he's wrapped in a blanket—a real one, not the ethereal quilt of armor draped over him by the blob—and the driver is saying something about evacuations, how Peter won't be able to stay at home. They'll check for anyone else still there but then they have to leave as soon as possible.

"Everything is going to be fine," Peter says, telling himself that, but the driver nods, vocalizes his agreement, and continues driving.

The calmness lasts until the car pulls as close to Maddie Smith's house as is safe and then Peter is afraid again.

***

Maddie and Brandon have been praying for hours, it seems. Neither has removed their hands from David's head, not as he twisted in the air, bending so far that the tips of his toes brushed Maddie's wrists. They cried as they prayed, their tears sluicing off the congealing oil on David's head and sizzling as they hit the floor.

Maddie knew this was why Montoya, as willing as he was, eventually gave out. The demon drains your energy and entices you to concede. The demon offers respite but never rest or release. Only Heavenly Father has the true rest. Maddie, however, was not ready to claim that reward and she would not let either of her sons give in to that temptation, either.

As his mother is tempted with relaxation—*has she ever had a vacation? No, because she must always care for you and your ungrateful brother*—Brandon is tempted with the baser fruits of the devil. He's seen it all before. Ruin has nothing new to offer him that the demon did not attempt to woo Brandon with the previous summer. Except for one thing, the thing that Brandon thought was safe last year: David.

I will kill him, the demon voice tells Brandon. *I will tear him apart body and soul right here in front of you and your mommy. And when mommy sees her precious little boy ripped asunder, she will relent.*

The voice quiets and Brandon sees exactly what will happen: Maddie sitting in a pile of gore that was David, cursing God for all pain of the last year, ignoring Brandon's pleas for her to step away from David's bodily remains. She does not listen to him. She grabs a shard of bone and stabs herself in the throat. She holds the makeshift blade and finally sees her living son. *Don't worry about the mess*, vision-Maddie says. *Nothing matters now.* She pulls the bone from her neck, dark blood gorging out of the hole. She falls forward into the mass of blood, bone, and entrails, bleeding out among the desecrated corpse of her youngest son.

She will die rather than live without him. You, well, she can do without you.

That's the button. Ruin did know Brandon's greatest fear. Their father left them and no one had yet convinced him it wasn't his fault. He couldn't protect his mother or his brother because he wasn't old enough for the higher priesthood powers. He couldn't be the man of the house when his own mother held higher priesthood authority than he did. If the fires swept down the canyon and burnt their house down, he couldn't save anyone.

He didn't matter to anyone.

As his hands begin to drift away from Maddie's, he hears a new sound. Not from inside his head or even inside the house. The sound is outside, it's a siren, interrupted by a honk and yell. Another voice answers back to the yell, and it's familiar.

"I have to go in and check, buddy. They don't have anyone else."

Brandon knows the man's voice: Peter Toombs, arriving just as Brandon and Maddie both crash from physical, mental, and spiritual exhaustion. The three Smiths all crash to the floor in one pile of worn-out bodies. Limbs entangled, no one is on top, not one is really on the bottom. It's easy to get lost in a dogpile like that. It's easy for one body, the smallest body, to slink away when no one can tell them apart.

CHAPTER TEN

"I have to go in and check, buddy. They don't have anyone else," Peter says, slamming the door shut behind him. The driver continues to speak but Peter blocks him out. The fire rages behind Maddie's house, the ash of forest and now other homes raining down. He shouldn't be here, but that is the story of Peter's life. Always in the wrong place and the wrong time with the wrong people. These people—this family—need him. What the black mass left behind pulses the message through his body.

Go! Run. Now.

He obeys, but even if he fought the command, his body would have gone anyway. The front door opens with startling ease and Peter is soon in the living room. The house smells like the wildfire smoke but also like something he's only read in other people's books: brimstone. A sulfurous aroma permeates the air, like a hundred eggs rotted and burst at the same time. He chokes on the smoke and the unpleasant perfume, but his vision is clear. He sees the tangled arms and legs on the floor: four legs, four arms. Someone is missing. He checks for breathing. Rhythmic pulls of oxygen from Brandon; short gasps from Maddie. Both are alive and that is good enough for now. But where is David?

Room by room, Peter searches. The wildfire inches closer and the sirens wax and wane, sounding miles away and right next door. "David? Where are you, kiddo? It's Peter. Come on out. We need to leave!"

The calling nets no results. Every door and cupboard is open. Peter opens the refrigerator, just to be sure. He sees a half-full milk jug, a curdled rime of spoiled milk runs along the center width. Once vibrantly-colored fruits and vegetables are molded, disintegrating, and black with rot. The back door is open and as Peter nears it, is propelled toward it, the doors and cupboards he opened slam shut at once, booming loud enough to wake the dead.

The crashing of doors and cupboards startle Maddie and Brandon from their stupefied state. The disentangled from each other, still expecting a third body to be in the heap with them.

"David!" Maddie screams as she grips Brandon around the waist. "Where is he?"

"I'll find him, Mom," Brandon says, needing to be valued, not like his vision. "Stay here and I will yell when I find him."

He's gone from the room before Maddie can protest. She does need him, more and more, because she can't do everything. She prays again, kneeling but instead of her arms like she's done her entire life, she lifts her hands to the ceiling, to the sky. Her head remains bowed, her nose pointed to the floor. A drop of mucus hits her chin then the floor. *It's blood*, she thinks. *I've cried so much that I broke something in my head.* But no, it's just snot. She doesn't wipe it away.

"God, I don't know why this is happening to us. I thought we'd beaten this thing. Please send help. I can't do it alone. Brandon can't do it alone. Send us someone to help." She persisted in her prayer, praying for assistance, for intercession. She prayed for Brandon and David, and Griffen and Montoya, as if they were saints who could whisper to Jesus Christ and tell him he needed to do something. She did not know someone was doing something.

David perched near the fence, hunched over as if he would soon spring on some unsuspecting small animal. Flames from incinerating homes served as a backdrop to the wicked smile on David's face. To Peter, he no longer appeared to be a young boy, but a vulture, snacking on carrion left by a larger predator.

"Hey, buddy," Peter says, slowing his approach. "There's a fire and we need to get out of here. Your mom and Brandon are waiting inside. How about it, huh? Let's get somewhere safe."

"Nowhere is safe," David says, although Peter could not see the boy's lips move. "Nowhere is safe with me."

"David, come on. Your mom is scared out of her mind and I'm sure Brandon is, too. So let's bail. Let's..." Peter pauses before taking a chance of language. "Let's get the fuck out of Dodge."

"David hates swear," the voice from the boy speaks. "But I don't. Swear more. Curse your God and Savior for me."

"God and I are just getting back on good terms, asshole," Peter answers. "I need all the grace I can get."

"Then you'll die and I shall be your ruin."

"Ruin? That's your name, isn't it?" Peter taunts the boy, skirting closer with every word. "What kind name is that? People like to see ancient ruins, but you are just some rundown, fourth-class demon that got beat by two old men and a woman. If Maddie was here right now, she'd kick your ass again."

David's body unfolds from the hunched position and becomes taller than Peter remembers. The clothes are stretched tight over limbs that do not belong to a preteen. Patches of hair have grown on the knuckles and knees, and a spotty neck beard has sprouted on David's chin. "I will ruin you, too, and end this family."

Opening his mouth to hurl more insults, Peter's voice cuts off. His jaw hangs down and his lips flap soundlessly. A rumbling starts in his stomach and the ligaments of his knees pull taunt as if he were a marionette, forcing him to the ground. The rumbling rises and he can feel his own energy coalescing from his toes to his gut and up his esophagus. He can't close his mouth and the rumbling forces a compulsion to vomit. He tries to hack the gorge out, but it refuses to work with him.

Relax. Just let it happen.

The voice inside him takes form. The blackness, the mass, the blob pours out of his mouth and nostrils. Inky tendrils seep from the follicles on his head, first looking like long strands of hair before melding with the glob from Peter's face. He does not lose consciousness. He feels the tugging in his body and the escape of the blob. He sees each piece fuse together into the chaotic form he first witnessed in the cabin with Wally Reins. Then the mass shrinks on itself, pulls tighter, finding form in the disarray. Legs mold, then a torso. Arms grow, still jet black, and a head. Hair, like the worms of black that grew out of Peter's scalp, fall from the top of the head in a shower of strange life, ending below the shoulders. The body is small, to Peter's surprise. He wants to greet it— now a her, he is sure—but still can't find words.

Beyond the congealing black mass is David and the demon Ruin inside him, extended beyond the height of the fence, towering over the roof of the house, taller than the inferno behind him.

"You don't belong here," intones the monster wearing a boy's face. "This is my place."

The blackness pulses as it—she—declares her stance. "I belong where I am needed."

Before the blackness attacks, Peter sees it for what it is. Some creature using the dark to hide, now taking the shape of the girl who drowned in Moon Lake. A ghost? No, not exactly. Peter still hasn't seen a real ghost. What he sees now is the form of a small girl rush toward an unnaturally tall creature that shares features with a boy not much older than the imitation girl. All sound returns to his mind. Howls of pain from both combatants, curses and oaths from Ruin, blessings and prayers from the girl-formed mass. He cannot close his eyes.

Brandon can't shut his eyes, either, although he doesn't believe what he is seeing. Peter Toombs lays on the ground, one hand reaching out as far as it can, his head rocked back so much that Brandon can see his tongue in the man's gaped mouth. He sees the conflagration barreling toward their house, leaving devastation in its wake. Between the fire and Peter, he sees David, quietly sitting with his back against the fence, eyes open as if in front of the TV, hands in his lap, a touch of a smile trying to find its way on his lips. The two bodies are stationary and hushed. If not for the roar of fire, the picture before him would be almost serene.

"Peter! David! Let's get out of here," Brandon shouts, breaking the stillness he believes is real. He gets no response.

Peter screams—he feels like he is screaming even though his vocal cords are shredded beyond use—at the girl because he knows she can't win against this beast. David has become something else, a being of pure spite. Vileness radiates from the enlarged body, but the girl does not relent. Her body morphs, becoming the killing mass again, covering the legs and waist of the demonic creature. As the darkness spreads across the beast's torso, Ruin's voice breaks. Peter can hear David again, begging for help but also guiding the mass to the vulnerable parts of the elongated body. Knife-like spikes of dark shoot up into the body's armpits and eyes, covering the rest of the body as it does. David yelps first with torment then victory. The body Ruin made crumbles under the pressure of the black mass and begins to shrink.

Peter bears witness to it all; Brandon sees only his little brother propelled unassisted off the ground then gently returned, eyes now closed, peace on his face. Maddie lingers in the house, deep in prayer. A triumphant blast erupts from the mass, heard by all even those who cannot see.

Finally able to move again, Peter stands and bolts toward David. His picks the boy up and then feels the touch of the mass. He turns toward it and watches the darkness fold and unfold on itself. It's no longer the little girl from lake, and then it is again. Mostly it is just the blob, the black mass that saves or destroys whomever it wants. And then, with one last unfolding, the darkness becomes light, becomes...

"Diana?" Peter nearly drops David as he sees that which he has yearned for over the years. Diana Ward, swathed in the crisp white of her wedding gown, all signs of the darkness gone. Tears well in his eyes and his knees weaken again. All the grief washes over him, but like a tide, quickly recedes.

No, Peter. The voice of the mass continues only in Peter's mind but it is as pure as fresh snow. *Diana has moved on. You need to let go now or you'll always be lost. You'll always roam and even I won't find you.*

"Who are you?"

Does it matter so much? Enjoy this moment because it won't last. Feel safe for now.

"That's not enough!" He can't hold back the tears, and his sobbing runs down his face and onto David.

It has to be. Now. Run.

The light that was dark dissolves. The image of Diana evaporates into the ether. Peter is left carrying David, staring into the house at Brandon. Maddie drifts behind her oldest, her face streaked with her own tears and runnels of mucus. She reaches out to Peter and David and roars...

"RUN!"

RUN.

Peter hears both voices. He focuses ahead of him and leaps the few yards from where he is to the back door. He trips, spilling David into the house and onto his mother and brother. His arms compact and break again. His left knee slams into a stone remnant of a walking path and splits. He repeats the command as the wildfire has caught up to him and the Smith house.

"RUN!!!!"

"We can't leave him, Mom," Brandon bellows. "We can't."

"Don't argue," Maddie answers, heaving the burden of David's weight and pushing Brandon out the front entrance. A rescue truck pulls in as they exit their house, barely occupied long enough to become a real home.

"Move it, folks, we need to race," says a man holding doors of the truck open. "Get in and let's get out."

The Smiths pile into the truck, not as tangled as they had been but with nowhere to get away from each other. The door slams and they speed away.

Behind them, the wildfire has taken over the house and the houses next to them. Roofs collapse and windows shattered. They escape the inferno but only they know how close to Hell they really came.

***

The sheriff lets Dale and Shirley watch the tape with him, just in case they can recall seeing the man on it before they came across his equipment. He's been informed by deputies that Peter Toombs' Mustang had been found not far from the shore of Moon Lake. The tires had been punctured and that was a concern.

"We've seen him," Dale says. "But just on TV. He's from around here, isn't he?"

"But you didn't see him at the lake the day you found his stuff," Sheriff Peery asks.

"No, and we told you that before," Shirley says. Her patience is gone, just like the joy of her honeymoon in the mountains. Even without this interruption, they had to get home. Wildfires on the other side of the canyon were getting out of control and getting back to West Jordan was sounding less and less likely. "We saw the tripod, then the bag and the camera. We looked around, but didn't see or hear anyone. We brought the camera right to you because we didn't want someone other punk to steal it."

"And you left this bag—" Peery picks up Peter's large camera bag, retrieved from the site, "just in case the owner came back. You didn't watch the video on the camera."

"Exactly," Dale says.

The camera is plugged into a laptop in the office. Peery would have preferred to watch it on a larger screen, but the office's one TV set was as old as his high school freshman daughter. He played it before deciding to let the couple watch it. Maybe a larger screen wasn't such a good idea, after all. He hits the PLAY button and watches Shirley and Dale instead of the screen.

Peter Toombs, black gloves and all, appears on the screen. He's talking about the girl who drowned in the lake and some people think haunts it, but soon the couple aren't listening to Peter speak. Their eyes focus on something behind him, something in the lake. It's dark and too flat and wide to be a fish; its movements are too purposeful to be driftwood. The mass rises above the surface of the lake and begins to form a column behind Peter. It grows and shrinks, appearing first as the shadow of a grown woman, then a small girl, and then…

"Holy shit!" Dale blurts out and Shirley reflexively smacks his arm, although she has the same thought.

The mass spreads like a bird then wraps its wing-like appendages around Peter. He continues talking as if nothing is happening. He is visible on the screen, although surrounded by this strange blob. As Peter signs off, the mass shrinks again, forming a basketball-sized sphere that hovers a few feet behind Peter then disappears as if it swallowed itself.

Peter reacts to a voice offscreen and the recording ends… until a flash of light like a quick overexposure replaces the static.

The sheriff doesn't look because he's already seen what Dale and Shirley are seeing now. A girl, maybe seven or eight, wearing what first looks like a nightgown but shimmers and becomes an old-fashioned baptismal robe, stares into the camera. She holds one finger to her lips and relays her message. "Shhh," the girl says.

NEXT SUMMER

An open notebook lay next to Maddie Smith's right leg. A pencil and a pen cozy up next to each other like old friends. A slight breeze ruffles the pages and most of them are filled with Maddie's crisp teacher's handwriting. She's written a title on the inner cover: *Tell No Man*. She's scrawled and crossed out and rewritten a dedication half a dozen times, adding a word, removing two, before settling on the simplest version: *For Peter*.

Empty bags from Walt's threaten to blow away with their hamburger wrappers inside. Brandon and David ate like teen boys do, quickly, somewhat slovenly, but also with gratitude. Every day is a blessing.

Today, Maddie and many others are in Memorial Park. Sounds of construction, the continued recovery from the wildfires that engulfed half the town, battle for supremacy over the guitars and drums of a band on the park's stage. The Atomic Blue's lead singer cajoles the crowd into buying t-shirts and stickers by reminding them all proceeds from sales go right into rebuilding efforts. She likes the band and she thinks Peter Toombs would, too.

From her blanket on the grass, she can see the band and her boys. They've grown so much, she thinks, but also knows they still have plenty of growing up to do. They are with friends, other survivors of last summer's fires. A tall brunette has her eyes on Brandon and Maddie tries to think of the girl's name, positive that she is a former student of her own. The name escapes her and she isn't sure if she will ask Brandon about the girl later or let him tell her in his own time. For now, she is satisfied with the smile on his face and that Brandon hasn't let David get away from him. Or that Brandon hasn't let teenhood or friends or that girl cause him to push David away.

At her other side is a slim blue book. There's a dog-eared page about halfway through and as she picks up the book, her finger slides naturally to that page. By now, she's read the book so many times she has it memorized. "There are some men who court Death and taunt it," she reads, not loudly enough for anyone else to hear. Or so she thinks.

"You, too, huh?" The ringing voice of a woman reaches out to Maddie. "Sorry to bother you, but that line always brings me to tears and makes me laugh a bit."

"Just like Peter, I think," Maddie replies.

"Oh, did you know him?"

"Briefly. Too briefly. I'm Maddie Smith." She produces her empty hand, amazed at meeting someone new in town.

"I think that's true of everyone. No one knew him long enough." The other woman accepts Maddie's offer. Her grip is tense but friendly. "I'm Debbie Ward. Pleased to meet you."

THE END
OF THE BLACKHAWK CYCLE

ACKNOWLEDGEMENTS

Thank you to everyone who has and continues to support me. It's been a wild ride to put this book in your hands, reader, and none of these things get done alone.

Thanks to my early readers Thom Carnell, Ryan Bailey, and Rob Erekson. Big thanks to Chip Erekson and Joe Johnson for being awesome people whom I can bounce ideas off of any time as well as commiserate about publishing.

Thank you those who had a look at this book in its early publishing phases: John Baltisberger of Madness Heart Press, Willow Dawn Becker at Weird Little Worlds, and Cody Langille from Timber Ghost Press.

While writing this book, I read a lot of Stephen Graham Jones, Agatha Christie, Neil Gaiman, some true crime, and scholarly books about movies (that's for a different project). I've been listening to Leonard Cohen, movie scores by Christopher Young, and Savatage. I also spent some time with the Mormon Tabernacle Choir. I did this for you. As always, I watched a lot of horror movies. I am grateful for all of these creative people who inspire me to get my own work out in the world.

Jerry Smith, you rock. Thank you for being a friend.

Thank you to Gabino Iglesias and Brian Keene for being mentors and examples of how to get along in this business.

Big thanks to Adventures Underground in Richland, Washington. Support your local independent bookstore. This is not the greatest acknowledgement in the world, but only a tribute to the greatest cover band from Payson, Utah, The Atomic Blue.

Michelle Butcher, one of my favorite writers and humans, was instrumental in getting this book into the world. Enjoy life across the pond!

My son Clark has proclaimed that he will be a writer and is working on a variety of projects. I am incredibly thankful to have him in my life.

What would I do without my wife, Savannah? She's the best person I know and keeps me grounded when my head is in the clouds.

And you, reader, thank you for going another round with me. Until we meet again...

September 26, 2022
Kennewick, Washington

ABOUT THE AUTHOR

T.J. Tranchell was born on Halloween and grew up in Utah. He has previously published the novellas *Cry Down Dark* and *Tell No Man*, the collections *Asleep in the Nightmare Room* and *The Private Lives of Nightmares*. He has been a grocery store janitor, a college English and journalism instructor, an essential oils warehouse worker, a reporter, and a fast food grunt. He holds a Master's degree in Literature from Central Washington University and attended the Borderlands Press Writers Boot Camp in 2017. In 2020, *The New York Times* included *Cry Down Dark* on its list of the scariest books set in every state in the U.S., representing Utah. Other work has appeared in the anthology *Humans are the Problem, Red Rock Review, Volney Road Review, The Inlander*, and *Fangoria*. He currently lives in Washington State with his wife and son. Follow him at www.tjtranchell.net.